HOLED UP

UP TO TROUBLE
BOOK 1

HANK EDWARDS

MITTEN GINGER MEDIA

CONTENTS

Chapter 1   1
Chapter 2   12
Chapter 3   20
Chapter 4   30
Chapter 5   37
Chapter 6   50
Chapter 7   60
Chapter 8   66
Chapter 9   75
Chapter 10   84
Chapter 11   96
Chapter 12   101
Chapter 13   105
Shacked Up   113
Shacked Up   114

About the Author   125
Also by Hank Edwards   127

SUMMARY

An FBI agent with an attitude about his assignment.
A civilian witness to a terrorist plan in need of protection.
A mole within the FBI ranks that endangers them both.

Civilian Mark Beecher overheard portions of a terrorist plot and is in need of protection. What FBI Special Agent Aaron Pearce thinks will be a simple babysitting job ends up more dangerous and life changing than he could have ever anticipated when an informant within the Detroit FBI office sends them on the run.

With no one to turn to, they hole up in a loft apartment and attempt to unravel the terrorist's full plan from the bits and pieces Mark overheard. Working together within the confines of the loft, the two grow closer and their attraction eventually erupts into passion.

But the informant is determined to find them, and when he does, Pearce is taken hostage. Now on his own, Mark realizes their roles have been reversed, and he is forced out of hiding—and his comfort zone—to try and save Pearce's life.

Holed Up is an opposites attract, forced proximity, FBI and civilian mystery thriller that kicks off the Up to Trouble series.

Holed Up ©2014 Hank Edwards
Cover design by Ron Perry Graphic Design
Book design and production by Hank Edwards
Editing by Sandra Rychel

First Publication, 2009

CHAPTER 1

"It's a fucking babysitting job," Special Agent Aaron Pearce snarled as he slouched low in the chair and put his feet on Assistant Director Harris's desk.

AD Harris stood up from behind the desk, pushed Pearce's feet off the edge, then sat back down. He folded his hands on the desk as he narrowed his eyes at Pearce.

"It's a request to provide protective service to a federal witness," Harris said. "And you will treat it as such. Is that understood, Agent Pearce?"

Pearce pushed himself to his feet and gave Harris a sarcastic salute. "Information has been downloaded, analyzed, and comprehended." He paused for a dramatic moment before adding, "Sir."

Harris stood up and pointed to the door. "Get the fuck out of here and book a plane ticket to Detroit."

"Detroit in February…" Pearce said as he walked to the door. "Thank you for the thoughtful winter vacation." As he left AD

Harris's office, he acted as if he was going to slam the door behind him but eased it quietly shut at the last moment. He paused to make sure he heard AD Harris call out "asshole" before turning with a grin to head to the travel department.

LATER THAT NIGHT, with his bag packed and his departure to Detroit set for eight fifty-five the following morning, Pearce decided to hit the bars. He made the rounds, spending some time at a few of the dance bars but ending up, as usual, at the DC Eagle. He knew he looked good: six feet four, 225 pounds of athletic FBI muscle, short dark hair, and dark brown eyes. He never had a problem finding someone to take home, and tonight proved to be no exception. A younger man with dark red hair cut in a flattop, a two-day scruff of red beard, and bright blue eyes started talking to him at the bar, and an hour later was following him back to his apartment in his tiny compact car.

The man's name was Ron. Pearce lied and told him his first name was Joe. Joseph, if he was in trouble. This line always got a laugh, and Ron did not disappoint. The kid was nervous, new to the city and the military/political secrets it held close to its dark, cancerous chest. Pearce was gentle with Ron at first, kissing him softly, helping him undress, giving the man's nipples little tweaks. Once they got past the oral sex, at which Ron was pretty good, Pearce let loose. He handed Ron a condom and said, "Put it on me."

Ron raised timid blue eyes to Pearce's face. "I haven't been fucked in a while."

"You haven't been fucked until *I've* fucked you," Pearce replied and gave the man a cool smile. "Put it on me."

Ron rolled the condom over Pearce's cock and then Pearce pushed him back onto the mattress. Pearce slicked up Ron's hole with lube, dipping his fingers in deep, then spread more on his sheathed dick. He moved in close, aiming the thick, blunt tip of his cock at the dark center of Ron's asshole.

"Ready for me?" Pearce asked in a deep, lust-filled voice.

"I...I think so." Ron looked up into his face, and before he could say anything else, Pearce slid halfway into him. Ron gasped, and Pearce pulled out only to plunge into the man again, burying his cock inside him.

And then Pearce fucked him, hard and deep. Ron could not even speak as Pearce slammed his cock into him over and over, faster and faster. Ron's legs bounced against Pearce's strong, sweaty shoulders, and Pearce felt sweat run off his face to drip onto Ron's red, upturned face.

"Oh fuck," Ron finally choked out. "I'm gonna come. Oh fuck yeah, I'm gonna shoot."

Pearce watched Ron jerk himself to climax and, moments later, pulled out of the man's well-fucked oc to peel the condom off and add his own cum to Ron's torso. Sweaty and spent, Pearce kissed Ron lightly on the lips before digging a cum towel out of the nightstand drawer to mop the man up.

"No, don't," Ron said. He mixed the separate puddles of semen and rubbed the stuff into his skin. "I want to be sticky with our cum for the drive home."

Pearce relaxed a little. At least the guy knew he wasn't going to spend the night all cuddled up close and dreaming of picking out a china pattern later in the week.

"Whatever blows your skirt up," Pearce said. He used the towel to wipe the sweat from his brow and tossed it on the floor as he walked into the bathroom to pee. "Not to rush you out or anything, but I've got an early flight tomorrow and I'm pretty wiped."

"Yeah, I understand," Ron called from the bedroom, and when Pearce returned from the bathroom he found the man already dressed and pulling on his boots.

"Thanks for a nice evening," Pearce said and, feeling awkward standing nude before the man, retrieved his briefs from the floor. "You're a hot guy. You'll do well in DC."

"Thanks, I had a good time." Ron stood up and kissed Pearce quickly on the mouth. "I don't think I'm going to shit right for a week, but it was worth it."

"You took it really well," Pearce told him, placing a hand on Ron's back and moving him slowly into the hall and toward the door. "You've got a hell of a hot ass."

Ron stopped at the door and turned to look back at him. "Well, have a safe trip, Joe. Where are you going?"

Pearce opened the apartment door. "Detroit."

"Yeah? Business or pleasure?"

Pearce gave Ron a look. "It's Detroit. What do you think?"

Ron laughed. "Okay, good point. But they've got some good sports teams. Well, two good sports teams. And the riverfront is nice."

"Yeah, I'll make sure to check those out while I'm there." Pearce put his hand on Ron's back again and eased him through the door and into the hall. "Drive safe, Ron."

"Maybe I'll see you around the bars when you get back in town?" Ron asked hopefully.

Pearce shrugged. "Maybe. Good night."

"Good night, Joe."

Pearce closed the door and threw all three locks. Yawning, he made his way into the bathroom to take a quick shower, his mind replaying the deep fucking he had just delivered to the poor kid. Ron had taken his pounding cock really well; he had to give the guy that much credit. In a way, it reminded Pearce of his time at the academy and the nights he'd spent with Morgan. As the water fell over him, Pearce's cock twitched at the memory of Morgan hammering at Pearce's own asshole, the man's dick pumping hard and deep with each stroke. Morgan had known how to plow an ass. Too bad he had been such a slimeball in all other aspects of his life.

Pearce took his dick in one hand and twisted his balls with the other, jerking himself off beneath the hot spray of the shower as he thought about Ron's hot hole. He kept his mind turned away from Morgan—that was old news—and finally, with a satisfied grunt, shot his load down toward the drain. He squeezed out the last few drops of cum, then soaped up once more and rinsed before shutting off the shower.

A few minutes later he fell into bed, the sheets still damp with Ron's sweat, and fell asleep in moments.

THE WEATHER in Detroit was as Pearce expected: gray and bitterly cold. The moment he stepped off the rental car shuttle, the wind whipped down the front of his leather coat, chilling him to the marrow and pushing a curse from his lips. He started the midsize sedan and let it run a few minutes to warm up, blowing into his hands and wishing he had remembered to bring his gloves.

The directions he had been given to get to the Detroit office of the FBI were more than fucked up. Orange construction barrels seemed determined to keep him from reaching his destination, and more than once he had to call the agent he was meeting, Malak Bata, for directions around closed freeway ramps and roads. How the fuck did anyone get around in this city? And it was called the Motor City for exactly what reason?

After a drive that lasted longer than his fucking flight, Pearce finally pulled into the parking lot of the Detroit office and took the elevator to the twenty-sixth floor of the bland building that may as well have had a sign out front proclaiming GOVERN-MENT OFFICES.

Agent Malak Bata was a Pakistani man, short and thin but with a fierce stare that told Pearce he was not a man to be crossed. Pearce felt underdressed in his jeans and chambray shirt as he followed the man through the office peopled with men and women in business suits, but then he decided that they had not flown to work from Washington, DC that morning, so if anyone had a problem with how he was dressed, they could go fuck themselves.

In Bata's tiny, windowless office, Pearce took a seat before the desk and the man folded his small dark hands on the blotter.

"Special Agent Pearce," Bata began in his crisp, accented English, "this witness you have come to protect and travel with up north is very important to national security."

Pearce held up a hand. "Whoa, hold up there, Bata. Travel with up north? Pardon me? No one in DC said anything about me taking this guy for a statewide joyride."

"No, you are correct," Bata continued. "And that is because we could not take the chance that someone in DC might be involved."

"Involved? In what?"

"In a plot to kill our witness."

Pearce sat back and frowned at Bata. "You're going to have to back up a few weeks, Bata, and catch me up."

"Forgive me. Let me start at the beginning. The witness lived in an apartment building in a downtown area of Detroit we have had under surveillance. The ventilation system in the building is old and allowed him to overhear several meetings that took place in another resident's apartment, a man for whom we have been searching for several years now, one Harold Hickam."

"Hickam," Pearce repeated and looked up as he searched his memory. "I know that name."

Bata nodded. "Most agents do. We have been searching for him because of his connection to a separatist terrorist cell known as the Kings of Rebellion."

"Okay, yeah, I remember that memo now. One of its outposts was raided and ATF found drums of fertilizer and a mound of cow manure they were using to make methane gas."

"Yes, that is correct." Bata sat back and steepled his fingers before him. "The witness, Mark Beecher, overheard several meetings with various members of the Kings of Rebellion. He also saw three men enter and leave the apartment at various hours of the day. He became alarmed and called Homeland Security. Mr. Beecher gave his statement, and the FBI was requested to stake out the building. We discovered one of the men was Harold Hickam and moved in to arrest him. Unfortunately, we missed catching Hickam, and instead we arrested two of his associates."

Pearce smirked at Bata's use of the word *associates*, as if the Kings of Rebellion were some kind of publicly held corporation. "Let me guess," he said. "One of them wants to make a deal. He'll rat out the rest of the Kings of Rebellion for a reduced sentence and some prison perks."

Bata nodded. "This man did mention he might be open to a deal, but not for the Kings of Rebellion. He has information on Harold Hickam's dealings with a member of the FBI."

Pearce raised his eyebrows. "Not an undercover agent?"

Bata shook his head. "No. Someone within the FBI has been leaking Hickam information, which is probably how he managed to elude us when we raided his building."

"I wonder how Beecher's information got past the informant," Pearce said.

Bata shrugged. "We have yet to get information of that level from the man."

"Okay, so Beecher is your only witness to these meetings, and he needs to be protected."

"Correct. The testimony of Mr. Beecher is crucial to keeping these men in jail and for our case against Hickam. Word on the street is that Hickam has gone underground but not left the Detroit area. The first trial for Hickam's associates is next week, and Mr. Beecher's testimony is key to the prosecution's case. For safety reasons, we are transferring Mr. Beecher to a small city north of here until then."

Pearce ran his hands down his face and sighed. "And I've been chosen to be his guardian angel for the week?"

"We could not risk assigning an agent from our office as we have not yet discovered the identity of Hickam's informant," Bata explained. "After I reached out to the main office, you came very highly recommended by Assistant Director Harris."

"Yeah," Pearce grumbled. "I bet I did." He got to his feet. "All right, I guess I should meet this great American hero."

Bata led Pearce down several hallways to a door at a dead end. Two agents sat outside the door, their suit coats draped over the backs of their chairs to expose their shoulder holsters.

The men nodded to Bata, gave Pearce a quick once-over, then got to their feet and opened the door. Pearce followed Bata into the small, confined space of a bland conference room that smelled of sweat and fear. A pale blond man with small rectangular glasses sat at the table, a yellow legal pad before him, pages of which were filled with cramped handwriting. Pearce was struck by how young and handsome Beecher was: twenty-eight at the most, with a square jaw and a day-old scruff of blond beard. The man shot to his feet, and Pearce noted that the tight black T-shirt hugged his firm chest and flat belly.

"Mark Beecher, this is Special Agent Pearce," Bata said. "He'll be accompanying you to the safe house."

Mark snorted a nervous laugh. "'Accompanying me'? Don't you mean forcing me to leave my job, my friends, my family—my entire fucking life—and move to the goddamn sticks because I overheard some terrorist asshole bragging about blowing shit up? Wouldn't that be a more accurate description, Agent Bata?"

Pearce raised his eyebrows at Mark's outburst and watched Bata carefully. The man nodded to Mark and replied calmly, "I know it seems extreme to you, but we want to ensure your safety, and this is the best way we know to do that."

Mark looked at Pearce, then back to Bata. "You think he's going to be able to stop Hickam's Aryan goons from killing me?"

"Special Agent Pearce comes highly recommended from Washington, DC," Bata explained.

"Well, bully for him," Mark shot back.

Bata continued as if Mark had not spoken. "These recommendations, coupled with the safe house outside of Wayne County, will, we feel, guarantee your safety."

"Oh, do you now?" Mark looked at Pearce. "So, Special Agent Pearce, have you ever gone up against a good old-fashioned, homegrown terrorist cell?"

Pearce stepped toward Mark and fixed him with a cool, vaguely angry look. He saw a flicker of fear in the man's hazel eyes, but it was soon replaced with a steely resolve that Pearce couldn't help but respect.

"Not terrorists, per se, but I've seen my fair share of dangerous situations."

"Great," Mark grumbled and picked up his legal pad and pen, then stuffed them into a soft-sided messenger bag. "And a dangerous situation to you back in Washington, DC would be what, *per se*? Politicians receiving blowjobs from tranny prostitutes in dark alleys?"

Bata opened his mouth to reply, but Pearce held up a hand and leaned in over the table to lock eyes with Mark. "Look, Mr. Beecher, you and I are going to be spending a lot of time together for the next week, got it? And when you think about it, I'm the only thing standing between you and a bullet in your head, so you might want to start being a little nicer and a lot more cooperative, okay?"

Mark's eyes narrowed behind his glasses, but he did not look away. He gave a quick nod, glanced at Bata, then back to Pearce. "Fine. Let's go."

Pearce stepped back. "After you, by all means."

Just as Mark got to the door an alarm began to buzz and a small strobe light high on the wall of the conference room flashed to life. Instinctively, Pearce grabbed Mark by the arm and pulled him back inside the conference room. He maneuvered the man out of sight line of the hall and cubicles outside and positioned himself in front of Mark, his gun out of the holster.

"Fire alarm," Bata said over the noise of the alarm.

The other agents, who had drawn their weapons as well, took positions on either side of the conference room door.

Pearce turned and looked into Mark's wide, terrified eyes.

"It's okay," he assured him, leaning closer to be heard over the fire alarm. "I'll get you out of here. Just stay close to me, okay?"

Mark nodded, and Pearce turned back to the doorway, his mind scrambling for a way to get them safely out of the building. The fire alarm going off just as Mark was leaving the security of the conference room was too convenient. The alarm would cause chaos throughout the building and allow anyone to get inside. It would also provide cover for anyone inside the office trying to get to Mark, like an informant for Hickam.

Pearce looked at the agents around them inside the conference room, all their faces tight with tension and eyes alert as they scanned the area outside the door. He knew there was a good chance one of these agents, even Agent Bata, could be Hickam's mole.

As the fire alarm buzzed and agents outside the conference room filed toward the exits, Pearce realized that, as of this moment forward, he was on his own.

CHAPTER 2

The shrill, sudden buzz of the fire alarm drove needles of icy fear into Mark's entire body, and he froze with one foot outside the conference room door. His stomach clenched, and he had just started to turn and look back into the room when someone grabbed his upper arm and pulled him inside. Pearce efficiently moved him out of sight of the hallway and up against the wall, standing in front of him and pulling his gun from its holster. Agent Bata said something about a fire alarm and then Agent Pearce turned his head, the man's dark brown eyes locking with Mark's for a moment, but that was all it took. Mark felt something stir inside him and stretch eager fingers up and out; something that, up until that moment, had been dark and dormant. It had been a long time since he had felt such a strong attraction for someone, and never this fast. He had kept any sign of weakness or insecurity sheltered from sight outside the walls he had built around his heart, masking the way in with sarcasm and a sharp tongue. He had been hurt so many times—most recently by Eric—it just didn't seem worth it.

Pearce leaned in close, and for a thrillingly horrifying second Mark thought the man intended to kiss him. But instead, the agent said loud enough for only Mark to hear over the braying fire alarm: "It's okay, I'll get you out of here. Just stay close to me, okay?"

Mark nodded, and Pearce looked away, scanning the room and the other agents. Finally, he heard Pearce ask Agent Bata, "Is there a freight elevator in this building?"

Bata nodded and motioned for Pearce to follow. Pearce turned and leaned in close again, closer than before, and whispered into Mark's ear, "Follow me. We're going to the freight elevator. If anything happens, stay with me, no one else. Got it?"

Mark shivered at the wet heat of Pearce's breath and cursed the swiftness of his erection despite the situation. He nodded and, adjusting his messenger bag to hide his condition, followed Pearce as Bata led them down the hallway, both agents with guns drawn. A few steps down the hall, Pearce turned and motioned over Mark's shoulder for the other two agents, the ones who had been guarding the door, to stay behind.

Mark followed Pearce and Bata through the crowd of agents and directors dutifully making their way to the exits. The fire alarm buzzed, and at certain spots along the wall, strobe lights flashed. They exited the office through a secured employee entrance and found themselves in the main elevator lobby. There were two stairwells in the building, and the evacuating crowds flooded both. Lines of vaguely anxious people had formed at each stairwell as they waited for those on the lower floors to clear out. Pearce reached back and grabbed Mark by the arm, pulling him along behind as he shouldered his way through the slowing crowd. Mark followed and tried not to think about the man's strong grip and how it might feel on his cock.

Around the corner from one of the stairwells, Agent Bata stopped at a large gray elevator door. "Here, this is the freight elevator." He pressed the call button and turned to find Pearce's gun in his face. "What? What are you doing?"

"Hey!" Mark exclaimed and tried to step forward, but Pearce held him back.

"Quiet," Pearce said without looking at him. "Bata, holster your weapon and step back from the elevator."

"He's been helping me since I came to the FBI," Mark protested, and Pearce grabbed him by the front of his T-shirt and pulled him around to press him up against the wall beside the doors to the freight elevator, never taking his eyes off Bata.

Bata raised his hand holding the gun and slowly placed the weapon in his shoulder holster. "It's okay, Mark. I understand what Special Agent Pearce is doing."

"It's nothing personal, Bata," Pearce said.

The elevator sounded its arrival and Mark jumped. Pearce pushed him into the elevator car and backed in after him, his gun still leveled at Bata. "I just don't know who I can trust around here."

Mark looked out at Agent Bata with wide, frightened eyes as Pearce pressed the button for the third floor. As the elevator doors closed, Pearce locked his gaze on Bata's and said, "I'll be in touch."

Once the elevator started to descend, Mark punched Pearce in the shoulder, but with his messenger bag around his shoulders he didn't get much force behind it. Pearce turned to him, brown eyes simmering with annoyance. "What the fuck was that for?"

"Because you're an asshole, that's what," Mark shot back. "You didn't have to point your gun in Bata's face. He was acting in my best interest."

Pearce shrugged and turned away, fixing his eyes on the floor numbers above the door. "I don't know anyone in this office. Until I'm working with someone I know and trust, we do things my way."

"Oh, and your way involves getting me out of a building that may be on fire by taking the freight elevator?" Mark folded his arms and glared. "Every third grader knows not to take the elevator when a building's on fire."

"Yeah? Then whoever tripped that alarm to rabbit you into the open wouldn't expect this move, would they?" The car stopped at the third floor, and Pearce slipped the hand holding his gun inside his leather jacket as the doors opened. "Come on. We need to be quick. Once we're outside, we're heading to the street, got it?"

"Why didn't you take us to the first floor?"

Pearce pressed the button for the first floor and pulled Mark into the hallway as the doors slid shut and the empty car descended to the lobby. "Because that would be the second thing they'd expect us to do."

They merged with the crowd in the stairwell, Pearce gripping Mark's arm so as not to lose him in the swell of people. Mark felt sure he was going to have bruises in the shape of Pearce's fingers on his biceps by the end of the day. On the first floor, they squeezed out the lobby doors with the rest of the office workers and stepped off the curb into the slushy mess of Michigan

Avenue. Mark followed Pearce as the agent trotted across the street and ducked into the lobby of a bank. They stood just inside the doors and watched people exit the FBI building across the street and make their way into the parking lot. A trio of fire engines pulled up, blocking the street and the exit for the parking lot, and several firemen dashed inside the building.

"Shit," Pearce whispered. "They blocked in my rental car. Fucking firemen, thinking they can just park anywhere."

"They are protecting people," Mark whispered back.

"Yeah? So am I, but do I get special treatment?" Pearce turned and looked around the lobby of the bank. "Uh-oh."

Mark turned to follow Pearce's gaze and saw the bank security guard giving them a long, cool stare. Mark whispered, "I think we should go."

Pearce nodded. "I think you're right. Come on."

They stepped outside into the cold wind, and Mark asked, "Now where? You just said your car's blocked in."

"I'm thinking on my feet here, okay? Just go with it." They made their way down the street to an intersection. A bus pulled up, hissing to a stop before them to deposit a group of senior citizens, as down the block a construction worker started up a jackhammer. Something small and sharp stung the back of Mark's neck and he winced, lifting his hand to the area and pulling it away to find a small amount of blood.

"What the fuck…?" He jumped as another bullet struck the wall behind him, fragments of brick again stinging his neck and the sound of the shot masked by the jackhammer.

"Get down!" Pearce shouted and pushed Mark down as he drew his gun. People around him screamed and ran for cover. "Get down! Everyone down!"

Pearce shoved Mark toward the entrance of an alley and stumbled after him, both of them staying low. Just inside the alley, Pearce pressed a hand to Mark's chest to keep his back flat against the building and turned to look into the street.

"Where is he?" Mark asked.

"I don't know."

A volley of bullets struck the sidewalk and wall at the entrance to the alley, and Pearce pulled Mark down to his knees, falling over him to protect him. The heat coming off Pearce's body surrounded him for a moment, and even as bullets chipped at the bricks and cement a yard away, Mark finally felt safe.

"Are you hurt?" Pearce asked once the shooting had stopped. He got up and pulled Mark to his feet. "Did you get shot? Are you injured?"

"N-no," Mark stuttered. "No, I'm okay. I'm not hurt."

Someone shouted in the street, and Pearce pushed Mark against the brick wall face-first. He then leaned against him, and Mark could hear the man breathing hard behind him, feel the wash of warm breath on the back of his neck as the round bulge of the agent's crotch pressed against his ass. Even as another round of bullets tore up the mouth of the alley, the more primal part of Mark's mind considered what it would be like to hear Pearce breathe like that as the man pushed into him.

"Okay, here's what we'll do," Pearce said. "We're going to run like our asses are on fire down this alley for as many streets as we can, and when we come out the other side we're going to take the first bus we see, got it?"

"Uh-huh," Mark replied. "Did you see who was shooting at us?"

"No," Pearce told him. "And I don't think we have much time. Let's go."

Just as they pushed away from the wall and turned to run down the alley, a car screeched to a stop in the street. A man wearing a ski mask leaned out of the passenger-side window and opened fire with an automatic weapon. Bullets zipped past them, kicking up garbage and shards of brick and mortar. Pearce threw Mark behind a Dumpster and fell in behind him.

When there was a break in the shooting, Pearce leaned quickly around the Dumpster, letting off two shots from his own weapon. Mark held his hands over his ears and squeezed his eyes shut. How the fuck had this happened? Sirens sounded in the distance, and Mark heard the screech of tires as the attackers drove off.

"We have to go," Pearce said and pulled Mark to his feet.

"But the cops are coming," Mark protested as Pearce dragged him down the alley. "They can help us, right?"

"Dude, you don't get it, do you?" Pearce snapped in his face. "You can't trust anyone anymore, okay? No one. Anybody we meet—FBI, police, elected government official, Martha Stewart, *anybody*—could be looking to have you killed. Got it?"

Mark pulled his arm out of Pearce's grip and turned to continue walking. "Yeah? So where in that category do you fall?"

"Somewhere between Martha Stewart and elected government official is my guess," Pearce grumbled.

They arrived at the opposite end of the alley and Pearce gestured for Mark to wait. The agent leaned cautiously around the corner and peered up and down the block. Two police cars sped past, sirens wailing and lights flashing, heading toward the FBI building. When they were gone, Pearce waved for Mark to follow and trotted across the street to duck into the alley. Once they were a few streets away from the scene of the shooting, Pearce stopped to reload his weapon, and Mark squatted with his back against the wall, catching his breath and trying not to shake.

"Look," Pearce said. "I know this sucks and it's nothing you asked for. I get that, okay? But here's the situation: Unfortunately, I'm the only guy you can trust right now. I may be an asshole, but keeping you alive is priority one for me, so we're going to have to find a way to get along."

Mark nodded as he rubbed his upper arm where Pearce had been gripping him. "Yeah, I get it."

"Okay. Let's go."

A cold drizzle began to fall as they turned and jogged off along the alley.

CHAPTER 3

Several streets farther, the alley ended at a side street crammed with parked cars and office workers hurrying through the steadily increasing cold rain. Pearce peered up and down the block, then pointed out a small restaurant with more waitresses than customers. They slipped into the smell of grease and fried foods and took a booth in the back. Once Pearce eased out of his wet leather coat, he sat with his back to the wall to keep an eye on the door. Mark grabbed napkins from the dispenser on the table to wipe the rain from his glasses.

"No bus?" Mark asked.

Pearce shook his head as he looked around the restaurant. "Not yet. I need some time to think."

Mark looked around. "So you chose a Coney Island?"

Pearce felt his eyes narrow in annoyance. "What?"

Mark waved a hand. "This place. A Coney Island." He tipped his head inquisitively and a drop of rainwater ran down his neck. "You've never heard of a Coney Island?"

"The amusement park, yes," Pearce grumbled, "but not a restaurant."

"Well, that's what this is. Greek food, hot dogs with chili and onions and mustard. Chili fries. You don't have these in DC?"

"Guess we're missing out," Pearce said. "Stop talking, please. Color on the place mat or something while I try to come up with a plan, okay?"

Mark frowned and looked through the menu, staying quiet for a few moments, then asked, "Do you think Agent Bata is really involved in this?"

"Don't know," Pearce replied with a sigh. "I just know I can trust only one person in this now: myself."

"Well, there's me," Mark said.

Pearce let out a quiet chuckle, then wished he hadn't when he saw Mark's hurt expression. "Sorry. You're right. We're in this together, okay? I get it."

Mark put his glasses back on and gave Pearce a long look, his hazel eyes seeming to drill right into his brain.

"What?" Pearce asked.

Mark shook his head and looked over Pearce's shoulder. "Nothing. I'll be right back. I need to pee." Mark got up, but Pearce grabbed his wrist.

"I'll go with you after the waitress comes up."

Mark sighed and rolled his eyes but sat down again. A moment later, a young blonde walked up with a pot of coffee. "You want coffee, guys?"

"Yes, please," Mark said, and Pearce nodded as well. She filled their cups and left them alone to look at their menus.

They got up, and once Pearce checked out the small bathroom, both men stepped up to urinals. Pearce tried not to think about Mark standing beside him, cock in hand, body coated with sweat from their narrow escape. He closed his eyes and willed the thoughts from his mind. He needed to stay focused if they were to get out of this alive. After washing their hands, they returned to the booth. Mark sipped his coffee and opened the menu again.

"How much money do you have?" Pearce asked, pulling his wallet from his jacket pocket and counting the cash inside. He had just over two hundred dollars.

Mark looked at him over the tops of his glasses. "Are you trying to tell me I'm paying for lunch?"

"No, I'm trying to see how long we can go without using a credit card to keep them from tracing our route," Pearce explained. "Now, how much cash do you have?"

Mark looked through his wallet. "Seventy-three dollars."

"Not a lot," Pearce grumbled.

Mark looked around and out the windows. "There's an ATM on the corner over there. They know we're in this area anyway. Couldn't we stop there and get some money when we leave?"

Pearce nodded and sipped his coffee. It was a good idea, but he didn't want the guy to know that. Pearce needed to stay in control of this situation. "Yeah, that might work."

The waitress approached, and Mark ordered a grilled chicken Greek salad. Pearce ordered a Coney combo with chili cheese fries. Once the waitress walked off, Pearce caught the expression on Mark's face. "What?"

"We're running for our lives, and you ordered a Coney Island and chili cheese fries?" Mark said. "Really?"

"Hey, we just got shot at, I'm going to enjoy what I eat while I can," Pearce replied. "Let me guess: you drink soy milk, eat only organic vegetables, and sponsor a baby gorilla in Africa, right?"

Mark laughed and shook his head. "No. I just thought, since you're in such good shape..." The guy blushed, and Pearce's gaydar perked up as Mark looked away and said, "I just thought that you would eat healthier, that's all."

Pearce grinned before he could stop himself. "Well, my doctor has been on me about my cholesterol, and I work out twice as much as I should have to because I eat so much crap. How's that?"

Mark tipped up a shoulder in a half shrug and sipped his coffee. "As long as you're happy."

"Well, I don't know if I'd go that far—" Pearce began but stopped when Mark's cell phone went off. The ringtone was some kind of electro-trance dance music shit, and it grabbed the attention of everyone in the place. "Turn that fucking ringer off!"

"I'm sorry," Mark said and fumbled his phone out of his messenger bag. He pressed a button and the ringtone ended abruptly. "I'm sorry; I forgot I had it set to ring."

"Set it to silent mode," Pearce hissed. "Now."

"Okay, okay." He pressed several buttons in a row and placed the phone on the tabletop. "There, it's off, okay?"

Pearce looked up as the waitress approached with their food balanced on her arms. "We need to not attract attention, got it?"

Mark nodded and sat back as the waitress placed his salad in front of him. She set Pearce's Coney Island hot dog before him and the plate of chili cheese fries in the center of the table.

"You guys set for right now?" She looked directly at Pearce as she said it.

He gave her a nod. "All set. Thanks."

"You let me know if you need anything else." She tore off their bill and placed it facedown by the fries. "Enjoy." She winked at Pearce, turned, and moved off, her hips swinging.

"Yeah," Mark said with an eye roll and bit into a pepperoncini. "We need to not attract attention."

"Shut up and graze," Pearce replied and took a bite of his chili dog. "I need to come up with our next move."

Mark's phone let out a loud single beep. Pearce nearly spit his food out as the man grabbed his phone and played with the buttons once more, all the while apologizing and explaining.

"I'm sorry," Mark said as he frantically stuffed the phone into his front pocket. "It's not the ringer; it was the voice mail notification. Okay? All notifications are off, okay? All of them. The notifications are dead to us."

Pearce stopped chewing and stared at him. He hadn't thought of the cell phone signal. Dammit, what was wrong with him? That was Eluding Capture 101. Any couch potato worth their salt knew that one. Their cell phones gave off signals that could be tracked even when they weren't in use.

He stuffed the last half of his chili dog in his mouth and said around the food, "Finish up. Now."

Mark looked around, his eyes wide. "What? Why? Is someone here?"

"Grab what you're not going to finish here and let's go. Now." Pearce got up, threw some cash on the table, and chugged the last of his coffee. "I mean it, we have to go. Right fucking now, Mark, come on."

Mark stuffed several pieces of chicken in his mouth and drank some coffee, then jumped up as well. His cheeks were filled with food, and he nearly whacked a guy in the back of the head as he swung his messenger bag up onto his shoulders.

Pearce stepped out into the rain and jogged across the street, checking to make sure Mark was still behind him before stepping up to the bank ATM. He slid his card in and requested the maximum withdrawal, swiveling his head to look up and down the street. Mark stood beside him, back to the wall, eyes watching everyone. Maybe the guy could learn to help Pearce keep him alive.

"Turn off your cell phone," Pearce instructed.

"I silenced it—"

"Turn it off," Pearce growled as the ATM churned out bills. "They can track a cell phone signal when it's on."

"Oh shit," Mark said and dug the phone out of his pocket. He shut it off and slipped it back into his front pocket again.

"Okay, your turn," Pearce said and stepped away from the ATM. He turned off his own phone while he waited for Mark to withdraw his maximum amount as well. Once Mark had pocketed his cash, Pearce stepped out into the cold rain again and headed up the street.

"Where are we going now?" Mark asked.

"Not sure yet. Just gotta keep moving."

Mark was quiet a moment, hurrying to keep up with Pearce's longer legs. "I'm guessing the safe house up north is out, huh?"

"Good guess."

"We need someplace to hide."

Pearce rolled his eyes. "You're preaching to the choir, Mark."

"Hey, this doesn't happen to me every day, okay?" Mark shot back.

Pearce nodded. "You're right. Sorry. Yes, we need to find someplace to hole up until the trial next week."

Mark was quiet for a few minutes as Pearce turned corners at random and kept looking furtively up and down the street, then said, "I know a place we could go."

Pearce stopped and looked at him. "Yeah? Anyone else know about it?"

Mark shook his head. "No. It's a friend's apartment."

"Forget it," Pearce said and started walking again.

"No, wait." Mark caught up with him and put a hand on his arm. "Listen. It's not like that. He's not a good friend. He's the friend of a friend of a friend, or something. Anyway, he's out of town on business, and I know where the key to his apartment is hidden."

Pearce narrowed his eyes. "Isn't someone checking the apartment? Feeding his cat, watering his plants?"

Mark shook his head. "This guy is a total narcissist—doesn't want anything else stealing attention from him. He has no living things in his apartment. He even has his mail stopped, so no one needs to pick it up."

A police car sped past, lights flashing, sirens screaming. Pearce looked around and shivered in the rain. They had to get off the street, that was for sure. And if they could avoid spending money for a day or two at least, they might be able to last the week on the two ATM withdrawals. Being able to dry out would be nice too. "All right. How far is it?"

Mark turned to consult the street signs at the corner. "About twelve blocks."

"Let's go."

BY THE TIME they stepped into the unsecured lobby of the converted warehouse, both of them were soaked through and shivering.

"I've never been this cold," Mark said through chattering teeth. "My bones ache."

"You're sure no one will walk in on us?" Pearce asked, then heard how it sounded and wished he could take it back. "We don't need any more surprises."

"No one will come by," Mark replied as he punched the button on an ancient elevator. The car whined and moaned as it lowered to the lobby, and the unoiled door shrieked when it slid open.

"Welcome to the slaughter house," Pearce grumbled but stepped into the car behind Mark, who hit the button for the third floor. "Third floor is good. Harder to get to the windows."

"He doesn't have much of a view," Mark explained and fidgeted as they listened to the elevator motor squeak. Pearce thought Mark seemed nervous, and wondered about the relationship between him and the owner of this supposed safe place.

"How do you know this guy again?" Pearce asked just as the door squealed open. At least they would know if anyone was coming via the elevator to kill them.

"He's a friend of a friend of a friend, that kind of thing." Mark glanced up and down the hallway, and Pearce followed his gaze. There were four doors along the hall, two across from each other at separate ends of the building. Mark stepped up to a fire hose inside a glass cabinet and eased the door open. Reaching into the wound-up hose, he flashed Pearce a smile that, despite his cold, wet condition, shot a quicksilver bolt of testosterone to his nuts, and Pearce felt something he had abandoned long ago shift deep inside him—something soft and lonely that longed to see Mark smile that way for him, and him alone.

"Bingo," Mark whispered and extracted a small ring with two keys.

Pearce cleared his throat and looked away. "And if this guy is just a friend of a friend of a friend, how do you know where he hides his spare keys?" Pearce glanced back at Mark, trying to read his expression and telling himself he was asking for safety and not personal reasons.

Mark stepped to the door across the hall and unlocked two dead bolts and a lock in the knob. He turned back to Pearce as he pushed the door open. "I was with the right friend one time when he needed to get in."

"Uh-huh." Pearce drew his gun and held Mark back as he leaned inside the door and looked around. It was a long, open loft apartment, dark with shadows. "Anyone home?" he called. There was no answer, so they stepped inside and closed the door behind them.

"Well, what do you think?" Mark asked as he dropped his messenger bag beside the door and slipped out of his wet coat.

Pearce looked around the dim apartment until he found a light switch. Flicking the switch brought an overhead string of track lights to life, and revealed in the soft glow was a comfortably furnished loft with sofas, armchairs, mismatched tables, a workout area in a corner by the windows, a kitchen area with stools at a granite-topped counter, and a big-screen plasma TV hanging on a brick wall. A Chinese privacy screen decorated with dragons and palaces hid the far section from the living area.

"You know some rich friends," Pearce said.

Mark shrugged and kicked off his shoes by the door. "Don't know him very well, just—"

"Yeah, yeah," Pearce interrupted, "I know, a friend of a friend of a friend." He bolted the door behind them, kicked off his own shoes, and shrugged out of his coat.

The loft was cold, and Pearce noticed Mark knew right where the thermostat was located and understood the digital programming well enough to turn on the heat. Moments later warm air flowed through the vents around the loft, and Mark ducked into the bathroom. Left on his own for a few minutes, Pearce padded around in his bare feet, shivering and checking the place out. He looked behind the Chinese privacy screen to find a tidy bedroom area. A king-size bed, dresser, and a tall armoire made of cedar were arranged in the area, and on top of the dresser sat a small plasma TV and DVD player. Pearce checked under the bed and pulled out two plastic bins filled with gay-porn DVDs. He noted some of the titles matched those in his own collection, though he didn't have nearly as many. Interesting, and apparently his gaydar had been on track about Mark. Or maybe not. Lots of straight single men have gay friends these days.

Mark opened the bathroom door, and Pearce slid the bins back beneath the bed as he heard him approaching the bedroom area. Moving quickly, Pearce pulled open some drawers and started taking out clothing for them to change into.

CHAPTER 4

Mark stared at his pale reflection in the bathroom mirror and tried not to think back on all the nights he had spent in this loft. He had not really *lied* to Agent Pearce about the loft owner being just "a friend of a friend of a friend." He had met Eric through a friend of his friend Calvin, scoring an invitation to Eric's legendary Halloween bash two years ago by being in the right place when Calvin's friend was drunk enough to invite anyone to the party.

Despite the stress of the situation, Mark grinned as he recalled showing up at the party with Calvin, the two of them dressed as "Laverne" and "Shirley" from the popular '70s TV show. The loft had been packed with people, mostly men, and the music had been loud, lights flashing, and the alcohol and drugs flowing. Mark, dressed as "Shirley," stayed closed to Calvin the whole night, overwhelmed by the number of people and ongoing sex acts he glimpsed happening in the corners. Later there had been a costume contest judged by Eric himself, in all his drunken glory. Mark and Calvin had won an elaborately named prize, something like "Most Popular Crossdressing Pairs Costume Based on Old Television Shows," which got them each a gift card to the Somerset Collection, the area shopping mall with the most high-end stores in the entire state. But more importantly, it had been a way for Mark to catch Eric's attention.

"And the rest, as they say, is history," Mark whispered to himself, then shook the memories away and turned on the hot water to wash his face. He would shower in a few minutes, but for now he and Pearce needed to change into dry clothes and get some food.

He was about to open the bathroom door when he stopped, hand on the knob, and looked back at the countertop. A nearly empty bottle of cologne stood off in the corner, Eric's scent, and Mark stared at it for a long moment, fighting his inner urge. Finally, with a sigh, he gave in and moved back to the sink where he picked up the bottle, removed the cap, and waved the open neck beneath his nose. The aroma was familiar, but instead of turning him on, it made him angry instead. There were some good memories he had with Eric. He could recall Eric's face hovering above him as the man slowly slid inside him the first time. A winter's weekend spent in bed, alternately watching the snow fall and having sex, stopping only to order food from the Chinese restaurant down the block. Or the time Eric brazenly kissed him in the middle of the Eastern Market while they shopped for vegetables, and the frightening thrill that went up Mark's spine.

But those moments were few and far between. The relationship had soured long before it had ended, and being here again wasn't triggering any kind of desire to get back together with Eric. This was a safe house, and nothing more.

Mark replaced the cap on the cologne, looked into his eyes in the mirror, and said quietly, "Over, done with, gone. Move on."

Mark opened the bathroom door and, finding the living room space empty, headed for the screened-off bedroom area. Pearce was pawing through the drawers, leaving Eric's clothes in disarray.

"Looking for stuff to wear?" Mark asked.

"Well, I'm not going to sell it on eBay," Pearce grumbled. He tossed a pair of boxers and some thick wool socks at Mark. "Here, knock yourself out."

Mark grabbed the clothes out of the air and turned away from the agent when he saw the boxers were a pair he had been missing since he and Eric had broken up. He shook his head, tucked the boxers and socks under his arm, and stepped to the armoire.

"Maybe there are sweats or something in here." He pulled open the doors to reveal hangers draped with clothes. Beneath the hangers were stacks of folded pajama pants and sweats. "Here are some."

Pearce stepped up beside him and Mark picked up the fresh smell of his sweat. A flush of attraction rushed through him, and feeling the heat of Pearce's body right beside him, he took a step back to give himself some space.

"Look at that," Pearce said, turning narrowed eyes to him. "Piles of sweats. Right where you thought they'd be."

"It was just a lucky guess." Mark shrugged and turned away to hide his blush. "I'm going to take a quick shower."

"Yeah, okay," Pearce said and crouched to select some sweats for himself.

In the shower, Mark turned up the hot water and stood beneath the spray, sighing as the chill finally released its hold on his bones. As he lathered up with Eric's body wash, his cock responded quickly to his lingering, soap-slick fingers, and he closed his eyes as he stroked himself. Memories of Eric merged with thoughts of Pearce, and before he knew it, Mark imagined himself straddling Pearce's hips, the agent's large hands moving over his body as his hard length slid into him. He could almost feel the subtle, delicious *pop* as the fat cockhead slipped past his sphincter. He could imagine the gentle force of Pearce's invasion as the man lifted his hips from the bed, and his own subsequent exhalation as his cock filled him.

Mark thought Pearce, as a lover, would be rough but caring. Whereas Eric had been sloppy and more than a little selfish, Pearce seemed to be an aggressively pleasing type who not only wanted to fuck someone for his own pleasure, but his partner's as well.

Mark could feel himself getting close to orgasm, and his strokes quickened as the hot water beat against the back of his neck. He pinched a nipple with his left hand, then slid his fingers down through the wet hair on his chest and belly to take his balls in hand. With his eyes closed, his attention turned inward, where he imagined Pearce sitting up and, still fully inserted within him, flipping Mark onto his back. Those large, strong hands gripped his ankles and sweat ran through the dark hair that he imagined covered Pearce's chest and belly as the man drove the full length of his cock faster and faster into Mark.

The bathroom door opened, and Pearce's voice, tainted with urgency, snapped Mark out of his fantasy.

"Someone's unlocking the door!"

"Fuck," Mark whispered. He could hear the agent inside the bathroom now and turned around to rinse the soap off his body. "Did you set the chain?" He tried not to think about the fantasy Pearce had interrupted, willing his erection to abate, but the man's proximity made it difficult, even with the danger of someone discovering where they were hiding.

"I did that after we arrived." Pearce paced the length of the bathroom. "I thought you said no one would come in here? I thought you said we were safe?"

Mark shut off the water and peered around the shower curtain, squinting without his glasses. "I'll handle it, okay? Hand me that towel."

Pearce looked at him, his gaze seeming to linger a moment longer than necessary; then he passed Mark the towel.

"Handle it how?" Pearce asked. "Hold whoever it is hostage?"

Mark dried off behind the shower curtain as best he could, wrapped the towel around his waist, and hoped it hid the lingering evidence of his erection. He stepped out of the shower and retrieved his glasses, wiping the fog away with a dry corner of the towel. "I'm going to tell whoever it is to come back later."

"Someone you might know?" Pearce asked. "I think you're keeping something from me, and if this whole 'keeping you alive' thing is going to work, we're going to need to be honest with each other."

Mark nodded. "You're right. Let me handle this and we'll talk."

Pearce stepped back and Mark left the bathroom, trotting to

the front door in time to see the last dead bolt turned and the chain stop it from opening. He heard a woman's voice in the hallway, the words foreign and tired, and he knew immediately who was outside: Marta, Eric's Polish housekeeper who came by once a week to dust and tidy up even when he wasn't home for a month at a time.

Mark took a breath and, lowering his voice to match Eric's timbre, said, "Marta, sorry not to tell you before, but I won't need you this week."

A pause from the hallway, and then Marta said in heavily accented English, "No work, Mr. Eric?"

"No, no need for cleaning this week," Mark continued. He could feel Pearce's eyes boring into his bare shoulder blades, and his erection threatened to bloom again. "Sorry, I forgot to call you. I didn't mean to make you come out here in the rain."

"Ah, okay, Mr. Eric," Marta said, and Mark could hear the frustration and disappointment in her voice. "No clean today. Okay, yeah. Bye now."

Mark stepped to his dripping jacket and called out, "Wait, Marta."

"Yes?" The woman's voice came through the crack in the door.

"Here's your pay for the week." Mark handed fifty dollars around the door, and it was snatched from his fingers. "Sorry again you had to come out in the rain."

"Oh, no trouble, Mr. Eric. Thank you. Okay. Thank you." Marta's voice was lighter, happy to have her pay without having to do any work. The door closed. Mark leaned against it with a sigh, then secured all the locks. When he turned back to the bathroom, he found Pearce leaning against its door frame, one foot crossed over the other and his arms folded on his chest.

"Marta, huh?" Pearce said. "Hungarian?"

Mark took a breath. "Polish."

"Ah, Polish." He looked Mark in the eye. "Care to tell me who Mr. Eric is?"

Mark sighed and nodded. "Let me get dressed." He walked past the agent, shivering at the flicker of body heat he could feel coming off the man, and stepped into the bathroom, closing the door so he could dress.

CHAPTER 5

Pearce knew he had walked in on Mark masturbating in the shower. The question was, who had the man been fantasizing about? Pearce realized there had been some kind of relationship between Mark and the man who lived in the loft. But he had also picked up signals that led him to believe there was an attraction between Mark and himself, and while that would lead to some obvious conflicts of interest, Pearce couldn't deny a growing desire for the man.

While he waited for Mark to dress, Pearce checked the refrigerator. It held condiments, several bottles of water, and a box of baking soda. That was it. The inside of the refrigerator sparkled, and Pearce decided that Marta did her job well while her boss traveled. He had been angry at first when Mark had given the woman the fifty dollars, but maybe it had been a good idea in the long run. She would stay away from the loft for the week and be happy she had been paid, with no comments to anyone.

Mark stepped out of the bathroom, toweling his wet hair. He

wore thick socks, a pair of sweats, and a thermal Henley that hugged his chest. Pearce thought about the blond hair that covered Mark's chest and belly, and wondered how that color would look around the base of his cock.

"Did you want to shower?" Mark asked.

Pearce shook his head and closed the refrigerator. "No. I want to know who lives here and what your relationship to him is."

Mark took a breath, then sat on the sofa. "Okay. Eric and I used to date."

Pearce moved to sit in the chair across from Mark. "Did you live here?"

Mark smirked and shook his head. "No. Eric doesn't like to be that tied down. We saw each other exclusively for about three months and then he broke it off."

"How long ago did the breakup happen?" Pearce asked.

"A year."

Pearce nodded but said nothing, and Mark sat back, his leg bouncing nervously. "What? Are you surprised?"

"What do you mean?" Pearce asked.

"I don't know," Mark said, his voice and posture defensive. "I just came out to you. Does that freak you out?"

Pearce shrugged. "No. Do you think your sexual orientation would matter to me?"

Mark shook his head and clasped his hands in his lap, lowering his gaze to stare at them. "No, I guess not. It's just... you always have something to say about everything."

"Always as in the last four hours we've known each other?" Pearce asked.

"Four hours? Is that it?" Mark said, giving Pearce a stony look. "Feels more like four years."

"Let's hope I can keep you alive that long," Pearce said, then regretted how it sounded.

That shut Mark up, and he simply nodded back.

"Look," Pearce started, then paused, debating with himself. Should he come out to Mark and relieve his anxiety, or would it cause more of a problem in keeping his attraction to the man in check? He took a mental breath and, clearing his throat, said, "I don't want you to be concerned with what you think is my opinion of your sexual orientation, okay? I'm gay too."

Pearce's pulse raced; he could feel the rapid beat of it in his temple. It happened every time he came out to someone, whether they were gay or not. Just saying the words "I'm gay" was a combination of a feeling of release at letting his secret out, and the knowledge that he had just made a statement he could never retract. There was no going back now. He had said it, and Mark sat silently across from him. "What, no comment?"

"No, no comment," Mark replied. "Thank you for telling me. Do you—is there anyone back home for you?"

Pearce felt a tired smile crease his lips and shook his head. "No. You?"

Mark shook his head as well. "No. I'm too picky, I guess."

"There's nothing wrong with that," Pearce said, locking eyes with him for a moment before clearing his throat. "So, will this be a problem for you?"

"What? You being gay?"

"No," Pearce said, and he could hear the sharpness of his reply in the single word. He softened his tone and explained, "I meant, will it be a problem for us to stay in this loft for a week? Will the memory of your relationship with Eric be a distraction?"

"Oh. No." Mark shook his head. "I'm done with that relationship."

"You're sure? Because I need your full participation if I'm going to keep you alive."

"I'm sure. Eric and I were… He was not the best partner."

Pearce nodded once. "Okay, I just had to check." He stood up and looked down at Mark on the sofa. The cleaning lady trying to come in the apartment had scared him, more than he wanted Mark to know. If something happened to him, Pearce needed to be sure Mark could protect himself. "Have you ever fired a gun before?"

Mark looked slightly scared. "No."

Pearce moved across the room and picked up his gun. He ejected the clip and expelled the bullet from the chamber as he crossed back to the seating area. "Stand up."

Mark got to his feet, his gaze nervous as he eyed the gun.

"Here," Pearce said, handing over the weapon. "Take it. It's okay, it's not loaded."

Mark took the gun in his hand. "It's heavy."

Pearce nodded. "That's because it's deadly. Don't ever forget that. Once you pull the trigger, you can't take it back. Got it?" Mark nodded at him. "Good. I'm not saying don't do it. I'm just saying that you have to mean it."

"Okay."

"Now, hold it in both hands." Pearce watched him but wasn't satisfied with the way Mark held the gun. He moved around and stood behind Mark, grabbing hold of his wrists to steady him. The clean scent of the body wash floated up to him, and he dropped his head, breathing it in, though he told himself it was only to sight along the barrel. He could feel the heat of Mark's body on his chest, and his cock stirred. He had to fight to keep from pressing himself against the round cushion of Mark's ass, from thinking about how it would feel to slip his cock between those firm mounds and into the tight, hot center of the man. After such a short amount of time, how could it feel this natural, this right, to stand so close to Mark?

Pearce cleared his throat, forcing those thoughts away as he spoke, his voice quiet, his lips right next to the pink curl of Mark's ear. "Okay. You need to relax. It will have some kick when you fire, so don't lock your elbows."

He worked with Mark for almost an hour, showing him how to load a new clip, chamber a round, and turn the safety on and off. He showed him everything except how to actually fire the weapon, for the obvious reason that they were indoors.

"Okay, I think I've got it," Mark said and slapped the clip home.

Pearce nodded at him, then stood up and walked toward the bathroom, pulling his sweatshirt off as he went. Halfway there, he stopped to fix Mark with a look. "Oh, and one more thing. I need you fully engaged in what we're doing here. While I'm protecting you, Eric never happened, got it?"

Mark's gaze jumped back and forth from Pearce's face to his bare chest, and Pearce had a pretty good idea it had been him Mark had been fantasizing about in the shower, and not Eric. Mark finally nodded and shifted position on the sofa to hide what looked like a sizable erection. Maybe being stuck in this loft together for a week wouldn't be too bad after all.

"Good." He headed for the bathroom. Looking back over his shoulder, he caught Mark watching him walk away, and said,

"There's no food in this place. Know of any take-out restaurants around here?"

Mark nodded. "There's a decent Chinese restaurant down the block and a pizza place around the corner."

Pearce shrugged. "Either one's good for me. Think about what you want and we'll discuss how to get it."

Once he was in the bathroom, Pearce leaned on the counter and stared at his reflection in the mirror still steamed around the edges from Mark's shower. Did he really want to get involved with this man he was supposed to protect? He had gone rogue from all bureau support and now he had come out to the man—this *gay* man—he was protecting. Pearce knew he was walking a dangerous line. It went against every oath and code of the bureau, but the attraction was there, on both of their parts, no denying it.

"Don't be a fucking idiot," Pearce grumbled to his reflection, and shucked the sweatpants to reveal his hardening cock. He turned away from the mirror and stepped into the shower. He tried not to think about the fact that Mark had just been in this same space, nude, stroking his own erection and, more than likely, thinking of him.

With more restraint than usual when he was aroused, Pearce ignored his yearnings and lathered up. He avoided touching himself as he rinsed off, busying his hands with washing his hair instead, and after rinsing out the shampoo, stood for a moment beneath the hot spray, pointedly ignoring his insistent hard-on. He needed to stay sharp, focused, to keep Mark alive.

Stepping out of the shower, he toweled off and dressed in the sweats bought and worn by the man who had loved and left Mark. He didn't like having to wear Eric's clothes but decided not to dwell on it and hung the towel on the rack, then stepped out of the bathroom. Mark was sitting on the couch, feet up on the table before him, scrolling through TV channels.

"Feel better?" Mark asked.

"Yeah." Pearce nodded. "Warmer." He sat on the opposite end of the couch from Mark and turned his attention to the plasma TV on the wall. "We make the news?"

Mark punched a channel into the remote, and a shot of a local reporter standing outside the Detroit FBI office came up.

"…no word as to whether the fire alarm triggered here at the Detroit branch of the FBI is related to the shots fired around the corner. For now, the FBI is only telling us 'no comment,' but several witnesses in the area of the shooting tell us two men were seen exchanging gunfire with men in a late-model vehicle before escaping down a nearby alley. Police are still searching for the vehicle and the two men seen running from it. From down-town Detroit, I'm Earl Hydecker, local news."

Mark looked over at him. "Is that good or bad?"

"Good that there are no pictures of us," Pearce replied. "Bad that police are looking for us. The FBI won't share information with them in case they've also got someone dirty involved with Kings of Rebellion."

"You FBI guys don't share very well, do you?" Mark remarked.

Pearce gave him a cool look. "We do when it's important and warrants sharing."

Mark saluted him and looked away, and Pearce thought back to the sarcastic salute he had given Assistant Director Harris back in Washington just the day before. Maybe he and Mark were more alike than either of them realized.

"After I get the food, we need to talk about what you over-heard from the Kings of Rebellion conversations," Pearce said. "Maybe we can figure out something to use as leverage to keep you safe."

"Leverage?"

"Yeah, just in case they catch up to us." Pearce got off the couch. "So what did you decide for dinner?"

"Chinese. It's good, cheap, and close by. They could deliver, or we could go get it."

"No deliveries," Pearce said and stalked to the windows to peer out at the darkening sky. "Are there blinds for these windows?"

"Um, I know there are blinds in the bedroom area," Mark replied. "Not sure about the windows in here."

They checked the windows and found blind cords for all of them. Pearce lowered the bamboo blinds over each window, then went around and turned on as many lights as he could locate.

Mark watched him switching on lights. "The bogeyman join the Kings of Rebellion too?"

"Ha-ha. I'm going to check something when I go out to get the food." Pearce looked at Mark over his shoulder. "That's your cue to place the order."

"Yep, right." Mark turned to rummage through a drawer in the kitchen until he found a take-out menu. "Okay, so what do you like? Almond chicken? Beef with broccoli? Chow mein?"

"Chicken chop suey with white rice," Pearce said as he checked his shoes and found them still soaked from the rain. "Wonton soup. Two egg rolls." He felt his socks and found them slightly damp. *Ugh,* he didn't want to put his warm, dry feet back into damp socks and wet shoes.

"Hey," Pearce called to Mark, who had just hung up the phone after placing their order. "What size shoe does Eric wear?"

Mark shrugged. "I don't know. Why?"

Pearce walked past him without answering and pulled open the armoire. He picked up a hiking boot and checked the size inside: 9. No way his size 10 1/2 feet were going to fit in them. Wet socks and shoes it was. He turned to find Mark watching him from beside the Chinese privacy screen.

"Wrong size," Pearce said and, pausing on his way past Mark, looked down into the man's eyes. "Just for the record, my feet are a size and a half bigger."

A flush of heat colored Mark's cheeks, and Pearce moved on, crossing the room to lean on the wall by the front door and peel off his warm, dry socks. He flinched as he pulled on the cold, damp socks he had been wearing earlier and slid his feet into his wet shoes. Better to wear damp socks out in the rain than use up the limited supply of dry socks from Eric's collection.

"That's gotta feel pretty gross," Mark said. He had plopped back down on the sofa and pulled a fleece throw over his legs. Picking up the remote, he started channel surfing again.

Pearce pulled on his wet jacket as he glared at Mark. "Are you comfortable?"

Mark looked at him and nodded. "Very."

"Good. Wouldn't want the star witness to catch a chill."

"I can feel the sincerity dripping from your every word." Mark grinned and turned back to the TV, and Pearce couldn't help grinning as well.

"Where's the restaurant?"

Mark pointed at the far corner window. "Go out the front

door we came in. Make a left, and it's at the end of the block on the other side of the street. The name is Phong's Garden."

"Phong's Garden?"

"Phong's Garden."

"What name did you put the order under?"

"Frank."

Pearce nodded. "Good. If you had said either of our names or Eric's name I might have been annoyed."

"Well, thank goodness I understand the gravity of the situation and realize no one is supposed to know we're staying here. I wouldn't want to annoy you." Mark narrowed his eyes into a soft version of a glare, then turned back to the television.

Pearce turned away to hide his smirk. Mark had a quick wit and was able to keep up with Pearce's sarcasm, and that was a trait Pearce had not been able to find in anyone he had met at the bars. He checked to make sure he had his wallet, then opened the door and said over his shoulder, "Think about what you overheard back in your apartment. And chain this door behind me."

"Aye, aye, Captain." Mark got off the couch and approached the door. "Be careful."

"You too. And listen, we need a code in case someone is with me when I come back up. Something easy that won't tip anyone off."

Mark thought for a moment. "Any suggestions?"

"The name of the place is Phong's Garden, right? So if anyone's with me and it's not safe, I'll tell you I'm back from Chin's Palace."

"Chin's Palace, got it." Mark looked at him, his eyes wide and scared. "So what do I do?"

"Is there a fire escape?"

Mark pointed to the window where the treadmill and weight machine were arranged. "Out that window."

"Make sure it opens and put your coat and shoes by it. If you hear me say 'Chin's Palace,' you run and get to someplace safe, okay?"

Mark nodded.

"If we get separated, go to the Coney Island where we stopped to rest. If I don't show up, find somewhere to hide and go back each day at three p.m. If I can, I'll come meet you."

Mark swallowed. "And if you can't?"

"If I don't show up by the day before the trial, then get in touch with Agent Bata again and arrange a meeting with just him. Someplace in public where you feel comfortable. Got it?"

Mark took a breath. "If you come back and say you have the food from 'Chin's Palace,' I go out the fire escape and find someplace safe to hide. At three p.m. every day, I go to the Coney Island to try and meet up with you. If you don't show up by the day before the trial, I contact Agent Bata and arrange a one-on-one meeting with him someplace I feel comfortable."

"Good." Pearce nodded. "Don't worry, everything is going to be okay, but it's best to have a plan."

"Yeah, I know. It's just...it's scary." A weak smile flickered across Mark's face. "So, be careful and come back soon from Phong's Garden, okay? I hear the food from Chin's Palace is crappy."

Pearce smiled, gave him a sharp nod, and closed the door, pausing to listen and make sure Mark threw all the locks. He took the stairwell down to the first floor to get a feel for the building, checking to make sure the door to the second floor was unlocked in case they needed to duck out of sight fast. In the lobby, he found a hallway that led to a rear exit, and he pushed through the door into an alley. The rain had eased to a cold drizzle, and he hunched his shoulders as he looked around. One stuttering sodium-vapor light threw a circle of illumination in the center of the alley, leaving each end in darkness. He let the door click shut behind him and tried the handle: it was locked. With a grunt of approval, he set off along the alley, his gun in his jacket pocket, hand tight on the grip.

Pearce crossed the street, and as he stepped up on the sidewalk, a taxi sped past, splashing cold water onto his feet and making him jump back from the curb. He sent a muttered curse after the driver, shook the water from his feet, then stepped into the noisy heat of Phong's Garden. The place was tiny, one of those take-out-only restaurants with the kitchen opened up right behind the counter. Three Asian men wearing sweat-soaked bandannas over their heads stood in a line, frying meat and vegetables in woks sizzling over open flames. Two girls ran the counter, collecting money and taking phone orders, shouting the orders in Chinese back to the men in the kitchen. He got their order, made sure that fortune cookies had been added, paid the bill, and stepped out onto the street. Pearce ducked his head, turning up his collar to try and deflect as much of the cold drizzle as possible.

He stayed on the opposite side of the street and stood across from the building to look up at the lighted windows covered by blinds. He could see Mark's shadow as the man moved from the kitchen back to the living room area, and a strange feeling of *home* washed over him. Pearce shook his head, slinging droplets of water from his short hair as he tried to dislodge the feeling, but it persisted, grew stronger even, and he cursed himself for falling victim to this weakness. He was on a job—a mission, if he wanted to glorify it—and he needed to stay focused and not let his emotions get in the way of his decisions. And he wasn't sure how he felt about being in the loft with memories of Eric lurking in every corner and pillowcase. Besides, hadn't he learned from his relationship with Morgan to not let himself get too involved with someone? He let out a rueful laugh as he thought that the FBI Academy had taught him a lot more than how to protect the country: it had taught him how to protect his heart.

A police car cruised by and Pearce ducked his head, checking the bag as if inspecting his order. The cruiser rounded the corner, and he stepped off the curb to jog across the street and up the steps to the lobby door.

CHAPTER 6

Mark could not shake the image of Pearce peeling off his sweatshirt and exposing his broad chest covered with dark hair. He was so turned on that his erection had yet to go down, and the man had left the loft more than fifteen minutes ago. Could Pearce have been coming on to him? Trying to entice him into sex?

"Chill out, Mark," he grumbled to himself and got up to get a bottle of water from the refrigerator. "Keep your head in the game. Pearce may be gay, but you're definitely not his type. He chases bad guys and carries a gun and does crime-scene stuff, and you…well…you chop vegetables and stir soup."

He sat on the sofa, then popped back up to his feet, unable to sit still for even a moment as his mind raced with images of Agent Pearce and memories of Eric. He had been surprised to step into Eric's loft and feel…nothing. Well, that wasn't entirely true; he felt an absence of feeling, which was actually kind of sad if he stopped to think about it. His relationship with Eric had been the longest one he had had to date. Shouldn't he have felt something when coming back into his ex-lover's home?

A few steps around the living room area brought him to a stop in front of the overstuffed armchair where he and Eric had last had sex. Mark ran his fingers over the smooth microsuede fabric, his mind turning back to the rainy night last year when a drunken make-out session had led to Mark naked with his legs canted back over his head as Eric, fully dressed, stood in an awkward crouch and fucked him with a rhythm bordering on spastic. Mark could still feel the uneven pulse of Eric's thrusts and the shallow breaths he had had to take because of the cramped position of his torso. Eric had come fast, plunging his condom-covered dick in deep and letting out a booze-tainted grunt.

His hand stroking faster, and on the verge of orgasm himself, Mark had gasped for Eric to stay inside him, just for another minute, but the man had pulled out and walked away. Mark's orgasm had dried up as he watched Eric's retreating back, and later, after Mark had dressed, Eric had told him he felt they should take a break and see other people. Once he had arrived back at his own apartment, Mark had taken a hot shower, washed the lube out of his asshole, and had not spilled a single tear over the end of his relationship with Eric. And now, back in Eric's loft, Mark decided that it wasn't Eric he missed so much as the idea of companionship.

Someone knocked on the door, and Mark's stomach tightened. He stood very still, pulse pounding and eyes wide as he stared at the door, afraid of what Pearce might say. Another knock sounded, more insistent, and Mark jumped. He moved to stand off to the side of the door.

"Who is it?"

"It's Pearce. I'm back from Phong's Garden."

Mark let out his breath and checked through the peephole to make sure, then unlocked each of the dead bolts and let the man inside. The smell of the food wafted in behind Pearce, and Mark's stomach rumbled as he engaged all the locks once again.

"Nice place down there," Pearce said. "Real homey."

"It's not much to look at, but the food's good."

"They should put that in the Detroit travel guide: 'Mark Beecher says the food at Phong's Garden is good.'"

Mark snagged an egg roll and took a bite. "Do they have Detroit travel guides?"

Pearce shrugged. "I dunno. I'm sure people come here. Detroit has two good sports teams and a nice riverfront."

They ate at the kitchen counter, perched on the padded stools, and Pearce quizzed Mark about the conversations he had overheard in his apartment.

"It was a long time ago," Mark said. "Over a year."

"Right after New Year's Eve?" Pearce asked, wondering briefly what Mark did on New Year's Eve and whom he had kissed.

"Yeah, the week after that. I was home during the day because my shift got changed around."

"Shift?"

"I work at a restaurant."

"Waiter?"

Mark narrowed his eyes. "I'm a station chef, but thanks for the vote of confidence."

Pearce shook his head. "Station chef? You cook in a bus station or something?"

Mark smiled. "No, but interesting guess. The station chef is in charge of a specific area of food preparation. There are sauté chefs, fish chefs, grill chefs, that kind of thing."

"What kind of chef are you?"

"Vegetable chef."

"So you chop vegetables?"

"Well, I do that, yes, but I also prepare hot appetizers, soups, pastas, and potato dishes."

"So we're eating take-out Chinese food when you could have cooked for us?"

"If there were food here, I *would* have cooked for us."

"Okay, good to know. Continue."

"So I was picking up around my apartment and kept hearing conversations, you know? I didn't really notice it at first, just thought it was someone's TV or something, but then I realized it was an actual conversation coming from within the building." He shrugged, embarrassed at admitting that he had eavesdropped. "So I stopped and listened for a while, just to see what they were talking about."

"You eavesdropped."

"Yeah," Mark said defensively, "and good thing, huh?"

Pearce grinned. "I'm not judging."

"Yeah, yeah," Mark said and waved him off as he ate some more food. "Anyway, I got the gist of the topic pretty quick. They were talking about the Oklahoma City bombing and how many casualties there had been and comparing that to September eleventh, and I remember feeling really scared all of sudden, you know?" Mark shook his head, his eyes distant as he relived overhearing that first conversation. He could once again feel the electric tingle of fear in his fingertips and along his spine, taste the copper in his mouth, and hear the phlegm-coated words of the man he had come to know was Harold Hickam.

"What'd you do?" Pearce asked.

Mark took a breath. "I didn't know what to do. So I just kind of put it off, you know? I was freaked out, and it didn't really sink in what it was all about until the next day when I heard them talking again. And then I started taking notes."

Pearce's eyebrows went up. "You wrote down their conversations?"

"As best I could. I lay on the floor by the vent and scribbled them down as fast as I could."

"Where are the notes?"

"I gave them to Agent Bata." Mark watched Pearce's face fall. "But I made copies." He got up and pulled the yellow legal pad from his messenger bag and handed it to Pearce. "The first ten pages are a copy of what I gave to Bata."

"Not a copy-machine copy?" Pearce said as he leafed through the pages of cramped writing.

"I didn't have access to a copy machine, and I wanted a copy for myself. So I just wrote it all down again freehand in that tablet." Mark picked up food containers and silverware and moved to the sink. Pearce started reading the first page of the conversations Mark had written down, and Mark cleaned up the kitchen.

After he had finished reading the pages of notes on the Hickam conversations, Pearce asked Mark questions about specific details.

"During this conversation about the target for their next attack," Pearce said, and Mark nodded, already anticipating his question.

"I know," Mark said, "it bothers me too. I came into that conversation late and didn't know what target they were discussing. They just kept calling it 'the target' and talking about scheduled departures, viscosity, and referring to hundreds, maybe thousands, of deaths."

Pearce clenched his jaw. "Dammit."

"I know. Trust me, I've beaten myself up over it time and again," Mark said.

"Well, it's not your fault." Pearce tossed the legal pad onto the coffee table and stretched his long, strong arms up over his head as he opened his mouth in a drawn-out yawn. "Sorry, Chinese food makes me sleepy. It's not your fault, though, you know. You couldn't know when you should have been eavesdropping."

"Well, I should have contacted the FBI sooner," Mark said.

"Yeah, but then Hickam would have bolted and we wouldn't have even this much information," Pearce said. "Remember that someone tipped Hickam to the bust, so he would have gotten away regardless of when you reported it."

Mark nodded and looked at the man. "Thanks, Pearce, I appreciate that."

Pearce shrugged. "Just tellin' it like it is."

They sat on opposite ends of the couch and watched TV, but Mark wasn't really following the shows. Instead, he caught himself looking over at Pearce quite a bit, wondering odd things, like what side of the bed the man slept on, what he looked like when he slept, and how aggressive he was in bed.

At one point, Pearce got up to get a bottle of water from the kitchen, and after sitting on the couch again, the agent held out his hand. Nestled in his palm were two wrapped fortune cookies.

"Choose your fortune," Pearce said, his voice theatrically deep and foreboding.

Mark hesitated, then picked a cookie. They tore the wrappers apart like two kids on Christmas morning. Pearce cracked his cookie open and pulled the tiny paper out of the crisp folds. He cleared his throat and read: "Someone nearby is thinking of you." Pearce smiled at Mark. "Aww, thanks. That's nice."

"In bed," Mark said automatically and felt an immediate blush tint his cheeks.

"Sorry?" Pearce said with a puzzled smile.

Mark rolled his eyes in embarrassment. "It's this thing my friends and I do. You're supposed to add 'in bed' to the end of your fortune."

Pearce read the fortune to himself and grinned. "I like it." He looked back at Mark. "But you're not in bed."

Mark blushed again and split his own cookie open. He looked inside, then back up at Pearce, his stomach tightening around the food he'd just eaten. "It's empty."

Pearce looked at him with such a serious expression, Mark almost gasped. The agent reached out and took the cookie from him, his fingers brushing Mark's palm and sending sparks jumping along his spine.

"It *is* empty," Pearce said.

"What does that mean?" Mark asked.

Pearce gave him a long, serious look that made Mark's stomach flip. "It means whoever was on quality control when this cookie went through was asleep at the wheel, that's all."

"Uh-huh." Mark turned his attention back to the TV and tried to forget about the empty fortune cookie and how close Pearce sat beside him.

Later, as both of them were yawning, Mark finally stood up, stretched, and said, "Okay, what are the sleeping arrangements?"

Pearce looked up at him through half-closed eyes. "I thought you'd sleep here on the couch since you looked so comfortable earlier when I had to go out in the rain, and I'd sleep on the nice, soft bed."

"Nice." Mark turned to glance at the Chinese privacy screen, then looked back at Pearce. "So what do we do? Rock-paper-scissors for it?"

"How about this," Pearce said as he stretched his arms overhead. "Since you already slept on that mattress so many times last year, you can have the bed and I'll stay out here on the couch."

Mark sighed. "Look, we could both sleep in the bed. It's big enough that we wouldn't even be anywhere near each other, so you wouldn't have to worry about one of my limbs straying into your territory."

"Did that happen a lot when you were sleeping with Eric?" Pearce asked.

Mark rolled his eyes. "Why do you keep bringing him up?"

"Bringing who up?"

Mark glared at him. "Eric."

"Eric?"

"Yes," Mark growled. "Eric."

"You don't like when I say his name?" Pearce asked, a little too innocently.

"No, it's not that, I just…" Mark fell silent. "It's just weird, that's all."

"What's weird?" Pearce asked. "Being here without Eric?"

"Oh my God, forget it." Mark got up and walked into the

bathroom, searching through drawers until he found an extra toothbrush still in its box. He opened it, squeezed out some toothpaste, and began to brush his teeth. In his reflection he could see the flush of frustration on his cheeks and wondered just why Pearce's teasing got to him. Was it the agent's unrelenting determination to throw his failed relationship with Eric in his face? Or was it the agent himself?

"You're going to brush the enamel off if you keep scrubbing that hard," Pearce said, and Mark jumped, turning to find the man leaning in the doorway.

Mark removed the toothbrush and said through the foam in his mouth, "Shut up."

Pearce chuckled and walked up to stand beside him as Mark spit. He could feel the heat of Pearce's body as the man looked through drawers until he happened on another unused toothbrush.

"Well, he's just a regular convenience store, your man Eric. Seems to me he's prepared for a number of overnight guests," Pearce said.

Mark rinsed his mouth and spit into the sink, then smirked at Pearce in the mirror. "Cute."

Pearce smirked back. "Thanks. I do my best."

Mark brushed past him and out of the bathroom. "Hey, Mark," Pearce called.

Mark stopped and turned to look back at him.

Pearce gave him a lopsided smile. "Sorry, maybe I went a little overboard with the Eric teasing."

Mark shrugged as the man's smile made his pulse pick up. "Well, thank you for saying that."

Pearce's smile widened. "Sounds like you stopped yourself just short of saying 'jackass' there."

Mark gave him a wide-eyed, innocent look. "Oh, did it?" He pointed at a cedar trunk against the wall. "There should be pillows and blankets in there. Good night."

"Good night."

Mark walked around the Chinese privacy screen and flicked off the lights over that section of the loft. He turned the sheets down, stripped to his boxer shorts, and slipped between the cool sheets with a shiver. He lay on his back looking up at the ceiling, just like he had so many nights last year, only now he thought about the man sworn to protect him and who would do anything to keep him safe, not someone who had most likely cheated on him and taken him for granted.

Mark thought about the sight of Pearce's bare chest earlier that day. He wondered how it would feel to have the man lying there with him, Pearce's broad, hairy chest pressed against Mark's back as they spooned and drifted to sleep together. Rolling onto his side, Mark pulled a pillow against him and curled up around it, sighing as he slipped into sleep.

CHAPTER 7

The next two days were a blur of boredom for Pearce. He liked to be active and the forced seclusion wore on him. Plus, unlike a house with different rooms to break up the monotony, the loft was just a long, open space, and the only place he could go for privacy was the bathroom. He read through the conversations Mark had overheard several more times but did not have enough local knowledge to decipher the target. There was talk of a scheduled departure date around Valentine's Day—which was three days away—as well as blast radius, viscosity, and a higher-than-expected casualty rate. He read the words again and again and questioned Mark about anything in Detroit with a scheduled departure time for Valentine's Day, but they both agreed that could mean any form of transportation: airplane, train, or bus. Viscosity could refer to the type of explosive they planned to use: fuel, oil, or napalm—hell, even liquid fertilizer had a viscosity.

Finally weary of reading the conversations, Pearce dug a pair of shorts out of Eric's drawers, stripped off every stitch of cloth-ing, and stood nude for a moment in the room where Mark slept. He looked at the pillow nearest him, imagined what it would feel like to be naked and standing beside the bed while Mark sprawled on the mattress, naked and inviting. His cock jumped and hardened in seconds, and Pearce grasped it tight in his fist. The Chinese privacy screen was the only thing separating him from Mark, and he could hear the man in the living room, leafing through the pages of a free local paper Pearce had picked up at Phong's Garden. But if he closed his eyes, Pearce could imagine him stretched out across the mattress, cock erect, eyes lust-bright. He could almost feel the soft heat of Mark's full lips on his mouth, nipples, and cock.

It took every ounce of strength in him to remove his hand from his cock and squat beside the bed. He didn't trust himself to sit on the edge of the mattress without lying back and giving in to his body's urge to release his sexual tension. Instead, he turned his mind away from the image of Mark on this bed, naked, warm, and hard. He thought instead about the conversa-tions he had just been reading, and after several minutes his erection subsided. Pearce got up and pulled on the shorts, followed by socks and his black Rockports, which had finally dried out after a few nights near a heat vent. He cursed the fact that his change of clothes was in the overnight bag in the trunk of his rental car, still in the FBI office parking lot. He decided against a T-shirt, more to see Mark's reaction than anything else, and strode across the loft to the workout area near the windows. He resisted looking right at Mark but felt the man's gaze on him as he passed through the living room area, and his cock twitched agreeably. He did a few sets with the weight machine, a series of lat pull-downs, triceps push-downs, and pec work. He pushed himself hard until he sat on the bench, sweat-drenched and breathing heavily.

"You okay over there?" Mark asked from the couch.

"I'm fine," Pearce grumbled. He got to his feet and chugged some water, then stepped up on the treadmill, feeling Mark's eyes on him and trying not to become aroused by the attention. He ran fast, faster than his usual rate, pushing himself hard to try to keep his erection at bay.

Mark flipped the paper closed and wandered over to the workout area. He looked up at Pearce still huffing on the treadmill and asked, "Mind if I work out too?"

"Free country," Pearce replied.

Mark walked behind the privacy screen across the room, then reappeared moments later wearing yellow shorts, white socks, and his running shoes. He was bare chested as well, and Pearce watched Mark cross the room, taking in the firm, flat torso covered with dark blond hair and the rounded bulge of his package hidden inside the shorts. Mark stretched for several minutes, combining traditional stretches with yoga moves, then changed the weight on the upper-body machine and began his workout. Pearce ran faster on the treadmill as he watched Mark work out, witnessing his muscles tighten and sweat bead up and roll down his sides. As he stared at the man before him, Pearce's breathing seemed to fall into rhythm with Mark's, and he could imagine the two of them entwined in Eric's bed, panting and sweat-drenched, Pearce pushing himself deep into Mark as the man moaned for more. He could feel the hot sweep of Mark's tongue as they kissed and see the dreamy fulfillment in the man's hazel eyes afterward.

Pearce shook sweat from his face and looked down at the treadmill's control panel. He was coming up on three miles and wanted to make it to five. Sweat coursed down his body, soaking his chest hair and drenching his shorts. He lifted his head and, to avoid staring at Mark, trained his gaze on the Chinese screen across the room, tracing and retracing the intricate dragon design that stretched across the material.

Mark let out a grunt that pulled Pearce's attention from the privacy screen. Mark's muscles stood out, glistening with sweat, and the ripe, masculine scent of the man stoked Pearce's libido. How was he going to last another five days with Mark in this space without taking advantage of their mutual attraction? He knew Mark was drawn to him, knew he could have the man if he made just one move, but he didn't want to complicate any further an already complex situation. And yet there was a part of him that looked forward to the next five days of forced confinement with a selfish glee. They were trapped here together: no one else could steal Mark's attention from him, and he could learn as much as he wanted about the man during this time.

Last night, sick of watching TV, Mark had suddenly shut the damn thing off and turned to look at Pearce's annoyed expression.

"What?" Pearce asked. "Did I misbehave? Am I being punished?"

"You can't seriously tell me you were paying attention to that drivel," Mark said.

Pearce had sighed and given in. "No, I wasn't. But what do we do now?"

Mark leaned back into the corner of the couch and stretched his arms along the back and the armrest. "We could talk."

Pearce rolled his eyes. "Oh yeah, that sounds fun. We could talk about boys and then do each other's hair and maybe get our periods at the same time."

Mark threw a pillow and hit him in the face. "Come on, Special Agent Pearce. Locked underneath that gruff exterior and icy stare is the casual, relaxed man you used to be."

"How have I given you the impression that I was ever casual and relaxed?"

"You could not have been this uptight your entire life," Mark stated. "Your asshole would have imploded."

Pearce surprised himself by laughing and, as Mark joined him, suddenly felt something loosen up inside of him. It was like being under water for a really long time and finally coming up for a deep, life-affirming breath of air.

"Tell me one thing you remember about kindergarten," Mark said.

Pearce furrowed his brow at him. "What?"

"You heard me: tell me one memory from kindergarten."

Pearce looked up at the concrete ceiling thoughtfully until he finally said, "Eating watermelon for a snack one day with Eddie Williams. We were both covered with sticky watermelon juice and seeds, and we laughed about that the rest of the year."

"See?" Mark had said. "I knew there would be something warm and sepia toned inside that thick skull of yours."

"Okay, your turn," Pearce had countered. "What's one thing you remember about kindergarten?"

Mark smiled. "The oak trees around the playground. There were at least a dozen of them, and in the autumn all the leaves seemed to drop at once, and we would make huge piles and run really fast and jump into them." He paused and looked off into space over Pearce's shoulder, seeing the memory so clearly that Pearce could almost see it himself.

"I loved the smell of those leaf piles," Mark whispered, and Pearce knew he was losing himself to the man. He had never even considered getting to know Morgan this well, and that had been his most intense, longest-lasting relationship to date.

They had finished, at two in the morning, with their senior years in college. Pearce shared a story about getting drunk at a house party and waking up in a cemetery, lying across two graves with an empty bottle of schnapps in his hand, a sour taste in his mouth, and a condom still on his cock, with no idea of how or why it had been placed there. Mark had laughed at Pearce's story and gave a long, rambling suggestion that Pearce had impregnated a zombie princess the year before—the only living human male to have done so—when he was a junior and had tried to be straight, and the resultant offspring had been so devious and vicious the zombies had made sure, in his senior year, to make him wear a condom.

Pearce smiled at the memory of that conversation as he ran and sweat streamed down his body. The zombie princess detail had been odd yet funny, and it made him smile every time he thought about it. He found himself looking forward to talking with Mark again that evening. What they would talk about he had no idea, but he found the man interesting and intoxicating.

CHAPTER 8

Mark stood beneath the hot spray of the shower and tried not to think about Pearce being in this same space just moments earlier. He struggled to keep memories of the agent's furious workout from bubbling to the front of his mind, but it was no use. Mark might as well admit he was intoxicated with the man, and who could blame him? The man had saved his life, was determined to keep him alive, was one of the most gorgeous men he had ever laid eyes on, was interesting, and seemed to be interested in him. *And* he was gay.

Water ran over his body, rinsing off the body wash lather. His cock stood at full mast, stubbornly demanding attention, but Mark would not give in to his body's base needs. Not with Pearce just outside the door, listening to the length of his shower and suspecting Mark was masturbating.

"Oh fuck." Mark sighed and turned around, tipping his head back and letting the spray hit him in the face. Why didn't he just make a pass at the man and see what happened? Well, one, because Pearce was way too butch to be interested in him, and two, if they were going to be stuck in this loft together for another five days, Mark didn't want to have to deal with the tension of rejection along with fearing for his life.

He turned his mind to the conversations of Harold Hickam and the Kings of Rebellion. Even more frustrating to him than the quickly approaching Valentine's Day deadline was the word *viscosity*. He was sure the use of it was key to their deadly plan, but what did it mean? His erection slowly abated with this new train of thought, and he shut off the water and grabbed his towel. Looking around, he noticed he had forgotten to bring clothes into the bathroom with him and rolled his eyes. Had he truly forgotten the clothes, or had he subconsciously done it on purpose? Either way, he would need to walk through the loft in just a towel until he could get dressed. He sighed and wrapped the towel around his waist, then opened the bathroom door and shivered at the temperature difference. His nipples hardened immediately, and he glanced around the empty living room area and kitchen as he moved quickly to the bedroom area, saying as he slipped behind the screen, "I hope you're decent back here, because I'm freezing and need to get dressed."

He stopped at the sight of Pearce struggling to pull a pair of underwear up his legs. The man's ass, round and pale beneath a fine layer of dark brown hair, caught Mark's eye, followed by the sight of Pearce's heavy balls swinging between his legs.

"Oh, I'm sorry," Mark said but stood where he was, eyes locked on the man's naked body, taking in the broad, smooth expanse of his back and the curved bulge of his biceps.

Pearce tried to step into the underwear, but his foot got tangled in the waistband and he fell sideways across the bed. The man cursed and kicked his leg out, sending the underwear flying against the wall. He laid on his side across the bed, nude, his back to Mark, panting and silent.

"Are you okay?" Mark asked quietly.

"You could leave, you know," Pearce said without looking at him, his voice defensive and cold.

Mark took a breath. It was the perfect time, but did he dare profess his attraction? What had Pearce been doing in the bedroom while he had been showering? Was it just a stupid coincidence that he had waited until Mark finished his shower to get dressed, and nothing more?

Mark decided to take a leap and, as his stomach knotted anxiously, said, "What if I don't want to?"

Pearce turned his head to look at him, keeping his body angled so the front half was out of Mark's sight. Pearce's gaze locked on Mark's, and he felt the tension in the room soar.

"I'll leave if you want me to," Mark told him. He hesitated, then loosened the towel and let it drop to the floor. His cock was filling out, sliding up along his thigh as it grew. "But I don't want to go."

Pearce was quiet for a moment that seemed to stretch out to eternity. Just when Mark thought he had made a mistake, Pearce rolled over and let him see what he had been trying to hide: the long, hardened length of his cock. "I don't want you to go, either."

Mark's mouth went dry and he felt light-headed, as if he had stood up too fast. Pearce lay before him, gorgeous and erect, his gaze moving up and down his body, lust smoldering in the depths of his dark brown eyes. Mark stretched out on the bed, and Pearce positioned himself so they were face-to-face. They embraced, Pearce pulling Mark against his hard body, the heat coming off the man warming him, baking into him, exciting him even more. Pearce's mouth closed over Mark's, and his tongue pushed between his lips. Mark groaned deep in his throat, and Pearce rumbled a groan in response. The agent's large hands seemed to be everywhere: clutching the back of his head, running along his arm to squeeze his biceps, caressing his waist on down to his hip, and seizing his buttock, kneading it with strong fingers.

Pearce broke their kiss and looked at him, bringing his hand up to place his palm against the side of his face. The agent stared into his eyes as Mark's heart galloped in his chest. "This could be a bad idea. You know that, don't you?"

Mark pulled him close for another deep kiss, his tongue soft and insistent. "Let's not think beyond today, okay?"

Pearce kissed him again, more urgently, and rolled Mark onto his back. He pressed his chest against Mark's, his tongue making slow, sensual circles inside his mouth as his hand slid down Mark's torso. Pearce wrapped his fingers around the base of Mark's cock and squeezed. Mark pulled his head back and closed his eyes, his mouth open to release a deep grunt of satisfaction.

Pearce moved his mouth to Mark's nipples, sucking and gently biting them into round, hardened points. He ran his tongue around each, wetting the areolae and dark blond hair that surrounded them. Mark lay stretched beneath Pearce, head tipped back, eyes closed, focused on the sensation of the man's mouth moving down his body.

Leaving a trail of warm saliva, Pearce slid his tongue into the valley of Mark's armpit, then down the center of his torso, cutting a swath through the hair and over the flat surface of his belly until he finally dipped it into the hollow of Mark's navel. Mark gasped as Pearce flicked the tip of his tongue into his navel, and Pearce tightened his grip around the throbbing shaft of Mark's cock, stroking it faster and faster.

"Oh God." Mark sighed and raised his head to look down at the incredibly beautiful man holding his cock and licking his navel. "That feels really good."

Pearce looked up at him and said with a devastating grin, "Oh, baby, this is nothing."

Then Pearce lowered his head and swallowed Mark's cock to the root. Mark let out a cry of surprised arousal, and his body jerked at the sudden wet heat of Pearce's mouth. Pearce held Mark's cock in his mouth for a long moment, his tongue pressed against the shaft, breath from his nostrils warm in Mark's bush. Slowly, Pearce dragged his mouth up the rigid length, pausing to focus his suction on the plump, supple head. He swallowed Mark whole once again, then pistoned his mouth up and down along his dick. Mark writhed beneath him, eyes closed, gripping fistfuls of sheet as Pearce sucked him hungrily.

After what felt like hours, Pearce lifted his head and looked up at Mark, lips swollen from sucking, and Mark said, "Get your cock up here." He watched as Pearce walked on his knees up the mattress, his dick bobbing in front of him. A long, silvery strand of precum hung from the fleshy cap, and Mark ducked his head, sticking out his tongue to catch it before it hit the sheets. He looked up along Pearce's muscular body to the man's face, their eyes meeting and holding as Mark raised his head, tongue still out and collecting the precum until he wrapped his lips around the hot, swollen tip of Pearce's cock.

"Oh fuck," Pearce gasped as Mark closed his mouth

around him.

Mark relaxed his throat and took Pearce deep. He pressed his lips tight around the hard, full shaft and slowly pulled back his head. Opening his eyes, he found Pearce looking down at him. Mark gripped the thick base of Pearce's cock, his fingers pressing into the dark bush surrounding it, and sucked the man fast and hard, unable to get enough of the cock in his mouth. Reaching between Pearce's legs, Mark fondled the man's shaved balls, pulling them down and massaging them as he continued to suck his cock.

"Oh that's it," Pearce said. "Pull my nuts. Yeah, just like that. Oh fuck, Mark, you're just starving for cock, aren't you?"

Pearce braced himself against the headboard and thrust into Mark's mouth. Mark laid still, mouth open as Pearce fucked his face. Pearce pumped into Mark's mouth, the plump head of his cock filling Mark's throat as Pearce drove it deep.

Mark released Pearce's cock and, still on his back, scooted himself down until the man's balls hung over his face. He grabbed Pearce's hips and pulled him down so his balls dropped into his open mouth. Mark suckled the large, smooth orbs as Pearce stroked himself and reached back to pinch Mark's nipples.

They shifted positions, lying on their sides across the bed in the 69 position, sucking each other and running their hands over their sweaty bodies. Mark moaned encouragement when Pearce reached around his hip and probed at the tight, furrowed muscle of his anus. The agent drilled his finger knuckle-deep into the throbbing center of his sphincter, and Mark gasped.

"Oh yeah," he said, pulling Pearce's cock from his mouth and stroking the slick length as he caught his breath. "Get that finger inside me."

Pearce took his mouth off Mark's cock long enough to wet his finger, then slid it deep into Mark's willing hole. The sphincter tightened around his probing digit, gripping it like a soft, rounded fist, and Pearce's cock jerked at the thought of fucking this man. Mark rolled onto his back and raised his legs, exposing his asshole. Pearce lowered his face into the damp valley of Mark's ass and ran his tongue over the sensitive ridges of Mark's anus. Mark gasped and moaned, encouraging Pearce to drill his tongue deep into the dark center of his asshole.

"Oh yeah, Pearce," Mark sighed. "Eat my ass. Get your tongue up there."

Pearce got to his knees and pushed Mark's legs up, lifting his hips from the mattress so he could press his mouth firmly against the twitching hole. Pearce bounced Mark up and down on the mattress, pushing his tongue deep into what felt like the center of Mark's being as he licked and suckled.

Finally, Pearce lowered Mark's hips and rolled to the side of the bed, opening a drawer in Eric's nightstand and pulling out a box of condoms and a bottle of lube.

"Every gay man uses the same drawer in his nightstand," Pearce said as he flipped open the cap of the lube bottle and slicked up his fingers. Getting on his knees, Pearce aimed his pulsing cock at Mark's full lips, and Mark opened his mouth wide to accept it. Pearce reached down and slipped a finger between the pale mounds of Mark's buttocks, sliding his finger in deep. He twisted it around to lube up the interior of Mark's passage, then pushed a second finger into him. Mark moaned around his mouthful of Pearce's cock as his fingers pumped faster.

Mark released Pearce's cock and fell back, stroking him as he lay gasping and groaning while Pearce's fingers pushed into him. Finally, Pearce positioned himself between Mark's legs and tore open a condom with his teeth. Mark watched him roll the condom along the thick length of his dick and slather it with lube. Pearce took hold of Mark's ankles, raised his legs high again, and looked down at him.

"Ready?"

"Yeah," Mark said.

Pearce kept his gaze on Mark's face as the broad tip of his cock pressed slowly into him.

Pearce paused, watching Mark's expression, and asked, "You okay?"

"Yeah, it feels good," Mark said. "Give it all to me. I want you inside me."

Using more restraint than he had in a long time, Pearce slid his cock home with a slow, steady pressure, and the hot, slick tunnel of Mark's ass closed tight around him. Mark dropped his head back as his entire length filled him, and Pearce paused with his cock buried to the hilt, studying Mark's face. This was different than all the other times he had fucked someone. He felt more than just a physical connection with Mark. The last few days in the loft had allowed Pearce to get to know Mark better than he had ever allowed himself to get to know someone before. He reached up and ran his hand across Mark's chest, taking in the sight of the man lying before him with his cock fully embedded inside him, fixing the sight in his memory to keep forever.

Then Pearce pulled his hips back and thrust forward again; before Mark could catch his breath, Pearce was fucking him. Pearce used short, fast strokes, spanking Mark's prostate with the plump head of his cock. Just as Mark's gasps started to come faster and closer together, as if he might climax, Pearce alternated his thrusts. He shifted from short and shallow thrusts to long and deep, then back again, changing the angle of his driving hips to keep Mark right on the edge of orgasm.

"Oh fuck me," Mark cried out. "Yeah, just like that. Oh God, I'm so close, you've got me so close."

Pearce picked up the pace and dropped his hips, angling his cock up into Mark's asshole, aiming for the sweet spot. He pummeled the man's hole, his hips driving now with a mind of their own, pulling Pearce after them in their race to orgasm. Mark's muscles gripped his cock and Pearce was so close now he was afraid he might come first, and he didn't want that. Finally, just when Pearce feared he might not have a choice in the matter of who came first, Mark finally toppled over to orgasm.

"Oh, I'm gonna come," Mark cried and stroked himself to a gushing climax. Semen splashed across his chest, some landing on his chin, and he lay gasping as Pearce plunged deep inside him a final time, head tipped back and groaning as he came into the condom.

Pearce fell on top of Mark, gulping in breaths, and slipped his cock free. Mark put his hands on either side of Pearce's face and kissed him as his semen smeared across their chests.

"That was amazing," Mark whispered. "I've never felt... anything like that."

Pearce nodded, still breathless, and kissed him hard on the mouth. He pulled back and said between breaths, "Me neither."

CHAPTER 9

Pearce lay next to Mark and watched the man's face as he slept. They had both dozed off after sex, and an hour later Pearce had awakened to the setting sun slanting through the blinds. At first confused, the memory of what had happened suddenly flooded him, and he rolled his head to the left to see Mark lying beside him, lips slightly parted, face relaxed and handsome beneath his sleep- and sex-tousled hair.

Carefully turning on his side, Pearce looked at Mark's profile and tried to commit it to memory so he wouldn't be caught staring at the man when he was awake. This was so different than any other time he had fallen asleep with a man after sex. Before, he had always awakened in a panic, wanting to escape, needing his space. But here now with Mark, he felt relaxed and comfortable, like his defenses could all be let down with no danger of attack. He couldn't ever remember feeling this way with someone, not even Morgan back at the academy, and he didn't quite know what to do about it.

Mark's physical presence aroused him, pulled him in, and made Pearce want to know more about him. The last few days spent with hours free to do nothing but talk to each other had broken down the last of Pearce's barriers, and he wondered if he had started to fall in love with the man. He had never expected to feel this way for anyone in his entire life.

Moving slowly, Pearce slipped out of bed and padded naked through the loft. He peed, then washed his hands and face. Mark's semen had dried on his chest, so he took a quick shower. When he was done and emerged from the bathroom, he found Mark sitting on the couch wrapped in a blanket.

"Oh, hi," Pearce said and stopped, one hand holding the towel around his waist and the other running through his hair. "I didn't wake you, did I?"

Mark smiled and looked away, blushing. "No, I just kind of woke up. I thought for a minute I had dreamed it." He glanced back at him. "But then I found your condom on the floor."

"Shit, I forgot to throw that out. Sorry." Pearce shifted his weight and looked around the loft as an awkward silence fell over them. He didn't want to say anything for fear of opening himself up too soon and scaring Mark off, and he had never been good at morning-after conversation. He had no idea what to say to the man, but he had every feeling in the world he wanted to share.

"So, I think I'll jump in the shower again too," Mark said and bounced off the couch, blanket still wrapped around him as he scurried past Pearce into the bathroom and closed the door.

Pearce smacked his hand against his forehead a few times, then retreated to the bedroom to dig for more of Eric's clothes to wear, noting that they would soon have to do some laundry. He pulled on a pair of sweats, thick socks, and a long-sleeve Henley; then, to keep his mind occupied as the shower ran on and on, he hit the kitchen and began to clean up: rinsing dishes and placing them in the stainless steel dishwasher, wiping down countertops, and rinsing all debris down the drain.

He heard the shower shut off and moved into the living room, fluffing throw pillows and folding blankets until the bathroom door opened. Pearce turned to look at Mark standing in the bathroom doorway, towel around his waist, his face a tortured mask of self-loathing.

"Hey, you need to know something," Pearce said, keeping his tone gentle.

"Yeah, I guess I do," Mark replied, and the hurt and sadness in the man's voice sent a sliver of ice into Pearce's heart.

"No, look," Pearce started, but then words failed him, so instead he walked up and kissed Mark hard on the mouth. He ground his sudden erection against Mark's thigh, and the man moaned as he pressed his own hard-on against him. The towel around Mark's waist fell to the floor and Pearce dropped to his knees, catching the bobbing length of Mark's dick between his lips and sucking furiously. He wanted to suck every bad feeling out of Mark through his cock; he couldn't get enough of the taste of Mark's skin, the sound of his groans and sighs, the feel of Mark's hands pressed against the back of his head.

Pearce took Mark's balls in one hand and reached up with the other to twist a nipple, all the while sucking his dick faster and faster. He felt precum soaking through the borrowed underwear and sweats he wore as his cock throbbed for release, but he didn't want to take his hands off Mark.

"I'm gonna—" Mark gasped, and his load exploded into

Pearce's mouth. The thick semen slipped down his throat, and Pearce hungrily sucked Mark's spurting cock dry.

Mark slowly drew his softening cock from between Pearce's lips and leaned down to kiss him. "That was amazing. No one's ever swallowed my load before."

Pearce gasped a laugh and pulled him in for another kiss. "I've never swallowed a load before. I just… I wanted to have something of you inside me when I left to get our food."

He kissed him again and stood up, looking down at the sticky, wet spot of precum on his sweats. Mark followed his gaze, and they both laughed.

"Let me return the favor," Mark said and knelt before him.

"You don't need to do this," Pearce said, but lust deepened his voice, and he could hear the lie in its timbre.

"Oh yes, I do." Mark eased the drawstring waistband of the stained sweats over the tented boxer shorts and leaned in to press his mouth over the sticky spot on the cotton of the underwear. Pearce sucked in a breath and tipped his head back. The strong taste of Mark's semen lingered on his tongue, and he savored it. Mark pressed his mouth against Pearce's hard length and blew through the moist fabric of the boxers. The damp heat of Mark's breath sent a shudder up Pearce's back, and he reached out to steady himself on the frame of the bathroom door.

Mark pulled the boxers down Pearce's legs and caught his dick as it sprang free. The wet heat of Mark's mouth engulfed Pearce, and he closed his eyes as his hips struck up an opposing rhythm to Mark's sucking. With a hand on the back of Mark's head, Pearce drove his cock deep into the man's throat. Goose bumps rose up on his skin, and he felt the familiar tightening of muscles as his release coiled in his groin. Opening his mouth,

Pearce sucked in a breath and, on the grunted exhale, thrust himself hard between Mark's lips as his orgasm burst loose. Mark swallowed every drop, his bruised lips nursing the swollen tip as he rolled his eyes up to meet Pearce's gaze.

"Oh, Mark," Pearce said through his breaths. "My God, that was amazing."

Mark pulled back from his cock and squeezed a final drop of fluid out of the slit, then leaned in to suck the head clean. Pearce twitched as Mark's lips touched the intensely sensitive glans.

"Tickles," Pearce said through a hiss.

"Oh, sorry." Mark gently kissed the tip and stood up. Pearce leaned against him for a deep, lingering kiss, tasting his semen and feeling his cock twitch. Mark broke their kiss and looked up at him. "This is not how I thought you would be acting today."

Pearce kissed him again and said, "I know. I'm surprising myself. But this just feels so right with you, I don't want to stop kissing you."

"I ordered dinner just before you got out of the shower," Mark told him between kisses. "It's waiting at Phong's Garden."

"Phong can wait." Pearce kissed him again. "He's got a garden to keep him busy."

Mark allowed one final kiss, then stepped into the bathroom. Pearce made as if he was going to follow him, but Mark stopped him with a stern look and a pointed finger.

"No!" Mark said, as though talking to a dog. "Sit. Stay."

Pearce grinned. "Don't you mean fetch?"

Mark grinned back. "Okay then, fetch dinner."

Pearce sighed, stepped out of the stained boxers and sweats, and rummaged in the bedroom drawers for more clothes. He found the last pair of sweats and pulled them on without underwear, then turned and headed for the door, stopping to look into the bathroom where Mark stood nude at the sink, washing his face.

"I'll be back in ten minutes," Pearce said. "Don't get dressed."

Mark shot him a narrow-eyed look. "Is that an order?"

"It is."

"Maybe, maybe not."

Shaking his head, Pearce walked out of the loft and hit the stairs, his cock bouncing nicely inside the sweats as a stupid grin covered his face.

Ten minutes later, Pearce stepped out the door of Phong's Garden and shivered. An icy wind blew off the Detroit River three blocks east, cutting through the sweats and biting his bare skin beneath. He turned his face into the wind, squinting toward the river as tears spilled out of his eyes. A big freighter ship sidled along the frigid waters, blocking the lights of Windsor, Canada, as it floated past, and Pearce wondered what it carried. He made a mental note to ask Mark when he got back upstairs, and turned away from the slow-moving ship to find a man standing before him. The man's appearance startled him so much, he jumped back a step and felt in his pocket for the gun, but the last few days had made him careless and he had left the gun upstairs in the loft.

"Whoa, sorry," Pearce said with a nervous chuckle. "Didn't see you there."

He went to step around the man but stopped when the stranger spoke.

"Got some Chinese food in that bag?"

Pearce stopped and looked up, recognition, followed by fear

and then anger, rushing through him at the sight of the man's face.

"Morgan," Pearce practically spit, and his hand curled into a fist.

"Easy there, Pearce," Agent Robert Morgan said and flashed the oily smile Pearce remembered so well from their days, and nights, in the academy. "Wouldn't want to get in a scuffle on the street. That could attract the attention of the police, and who knows where that might lead."

Pearce swallowed his anger, forced it into a corner of his brain, and tried to understand what Morgan's appearance meant here on the street outside the place where he and Mark had holed up. He took a step back, putting more space between them, and glanced up at the windows of the loft. He saw a shadow pass behind the blinds as Mark walked past the windows, and his heart stuttered at the sudden realization they could both be dead in a matter of minutes. He had failed, not just his job to protect Mark, but Mark himself.

"Oh yeah," Morgan said, pulling Pearce's attention back to his acne-scarred yet ruggedly handsome face. "You've been sloppy, old friend, real sloppy."

Pearce tightened his muscles in preparation of jumping Morgan, but the man must have sensed his tension and pulled a gun from his coat pocket. He held it close against his side opposite the street and out of sight of passing cars, not that any of them would care in this neighborhood.

"Don't be stupid," Morgan said. "Now, let's take the food upstairs to Mark, shall we? It's too cold out here for us to catch up properly. And we have a lot of catching up to do."

Pearce's mind ticked through all possible escape avenues, but each one would mean leaving Mark behind, and he couldn't do that. With slumped shoulders, Pearce preceded Morgan across the street. They entered the building's lobby, and Pearce turned toward the stairs, but Morgan called him back.

"I'm a little tired. Let's take the elevator."

Pearce pressed the call button, and they listened to the decrepit lift moan and grind its way down from an upper floor.

"What happened to you?" Pearce asked, his voice a low growl. "What made you turn your back on the oath we took when we graduated the academy?"

Morgan shrugged. "They made me an offer." The elevator arrived, and the door squealed as Pearce pulled it open. Morgan followed closely behind him, the muzzle of the gun jabbing into his back at the base of his spine. "Besides, have you ever talked to Harold Hickam?"

Pearce hit the button for the fourth floor. "No, never had the displeasure."

"Ah, ah, ah," Morgan chided him and reached out to press the third-floor button. "I've been watching you for two days now. I know you're on the third floor. There's a small gap in the blinds, you know. It's been interesting watching the two of you together. You seem to be getting quite cozy, but I'd imagine you're sick to death of Chinese food."

Pearce watched Morgan closely, gauging distance and the odds of getting to him before the gun went off.

"I know what you're thinking," Morgan said and pressed himself against the wall as the elevator lurched to a stop at the third floor. "But I have backup with me."

The elevator door creaked when Pearce pulled it open. He

flinched, then looked out at the hulking form of what was undoubtedly a member of the Kings of Rebellion.

Pearce snarled at Morgan. "I see your taste in friends has degraded since we knew each other."

"Pleasant, as always." Morgan motioned with the gun for Pearce to exit the elevator car, and he stepped into the hallway.

"No tricks," Morgan said. "We know which door it is."

"Of course you do." Pearce walked up to the loft door and raised his hand.

"Use the key," Morgan said and pressed the gun into his side.

Pearce flinched and clenched his jaw. "I leave them behind just in case someone with a gun takes me hostage."

Morgan considered this a moment, then nodded. "Knock. But no tricks."

Pearce took a breath and knocked on the door, hoping Mark would remember the signal they had worked out their first day together.

CHAPTER 10

Mark arranged plates and silverware on the coffee table and had just turned to go back for water glasses when someone knocked. He walked toward the door, wearing just a pair of boxer briefs, his cock hardening as he thought about Pearce's mouth, hands, and body. But the most arousing thing about the man was his eyes, those soft brown eyes that had drawn him in the moment Pearce had stepped into the conference room at the FBI office just a few days ago. Just a few days? Mark shook his head; it felt like he'd known Pearce for months already. He pressed his eye to the peephole and saw Pearce staring back at him.

"What's the secret password?" Mark said in a teasing voice.

Pearce didn't even crack a smile. "I've got the food from Chin's Palace."

Mark frowned. "Chin's Palace?" He put a hand on the top lock and was about to twist it open, the question *Where's Chin's Palace?* almost slipping free from his lips before a memory smashed through to the front of his mind. He froze and his hard-on withered as his stomach knotted with fear. "Chin's Palace" was the code that someone was with Pearce. They were in danger.

"Um, just a minute," Mark said, unable to keep the sudden quiver of fear from his voice. He backed away from the door, his mind frantically sifting through memories to find the one he needed. At last he found it and turned to look at the window by the exercise equipment. The fire escape. He was supposed to climb down and run, forget about Pearce, just get himself to safety and go to the Coney Island at three p.m. each day until the trial.

Mark thought he heard a small scuffle in the hallway and then Pearce knocked again, louder this time, more insistent.

"Did you hear me?" Pearce called through the door. "I said I've got the food from Chin's Palace. Stop fucking around, Mark, and get your ass in gear."

Mark heard the underlying meaning in Pearce's words: *run!* He took a breath, grabbed the pair of sweats and sweatshirt from the chair, and tried to keep his voice even as he called, "Sorry, just a minute. I'm a little indisposed at the moment."

He pulled on the clothes, jammed his feet into his shoes, which thankfully had dried out by the heat vent, and grabbed his coat and messenger bag. At the window, he took a last look around the apartment, then ran to the sofa and grabbed Pearce's gun from the table, stuffing it in his coat pocket and slipping out the window onto the fire escape.

All the way down the icy steel steps, Mark kept expecting to feel the sudden punch of a bullet in the back of his head. He tried to ignore the danger by focusing on making as little noise as possible, keeping his mind on his footing, but his heart was pounding hard and his breath rasped in his throat. Finally, he dropped to the ground at the corner of the building and pressed his back against the wall next to the gated parking lot of the building. Peering around the corner, he found no one on the street. He took another moment to examine each of the cars parked along the curb, but saw no one sitting in wait.

With a hand gripping the gun in his coat pocket, Mark hurried across the street and ducked behind a graffiti-stained clothing store. From this vantage point, Mark could see Eric's loft windows as well as the front entrance of the building. He worked on slowing his breathing and shivered as the cold from the brick wall behind him seeped through the jacket into his limbs.

A few minutes later, two men in camouflage jackets came out of the front entrance, hands in their coat pockets, heads swiveling up and down the street as if looking for someone. Mark inched farther back into the shadows of the building and kept his breathing slow. His legs were tensed, ready to take flight.

"He's gone," a deep voice grumbled, carrying across the street on the cold, still night air. "They must have had a code word or something."

"Interesting," another voice came to him, deep, smooth, confident, and almost amused. Mark leaned forward a bit to see around the corner. Three men stood in a loose group around Pearce, the two camo-sporting goons and a man in a trench coat with the hair and stance of a federal agent. Mark narrowed his eyes, trying to see the man's face better in the sodium-vapor glow of the streetlamp, but his features were indistinct. He could see, however, that Pearce had blood running from his nose and a small gash on his forehead. His stomach twisted at the thought of Pearce in pain—and all to protect him.

"Fuck," Mark whispered and turned away, fighting back tears as he tried to think of what to do. Even though he knew it would be the smart thing to do, he couldn't just run and leave Pearce to his fate with these men. They were terrorists; they wouldn't hesitate to kill him.

"Look, Morgan," Pearce's voice floated to Mark, and he held his breath, burning the name Morgan into his brain as he listened. "You're not going to find him, okay? He's on the run, and he's pretty good at keeping his head down. Plus, he's got friends all over this city. You're not going to find him before the trial, so why don't you do the smart thing and let me go?"

"Oh, Aaron, if only it were that easy."

Mark blinked and turned his head to look across the street again. Aaron? Was that Pearce's first name? Why did the agent named Morgan call Pearce by his first name? Did they have some kind of history together? He savored the information and said Pearce's first name like a mantra in the back of his mind as he listened to the conversation: *Aaron, Aaron, Aaron, Aaron.*

Morgan continued: "But you see, you're going to get to know a lot more about our group, and we won't be able to just let you go after that. So I'm kind of stuck here." He jerked his head at the goons in camo. "Get the van."

The men ran off, and Mark saw Morgan lean in close to Pearce and whisper something. Pearce lowered his eyes to the sidewalk and shook his head, then looked up to glare at Morgan. "Not a fucking chance."

Morgan shrugged and pushed Pearce toward the street as a

white-panel van pulled up to the curb. Seconds later, a car pulled into the gated parking lot of Eric's building across the street, snagging Mark's attention for a moment, long enough to see the Human Rights Campaign Fund and rainbow flag stickers in the back window. An idea struggled to life through his panic, and as he turned back to see Pearce shoved into the back of the van, he knew what he had to do.

Mark watched the van pull away from the curb and head down the street, stopping at a traffic light two blocks east. He noticed the right taillight was out, and then dashed across the street, sweaty hand gripping Pearce's gun, thinking that it was now Aaron's gun, and slipped past the gate as it rolled shut and into the parking lot behind the newly arrived car. The vehicle pulled into a numbered spot and the engine switched off. The interior light clicked on, and through the back window Mark could see the driver picking up items from the front passenger seat. He hesitated a moment, studying the young man's profile through the safety glass, feeling a wave of regret and exhaustion threaten to keep him from doing what he needed to do next. Thoughts of Pearce and the danger he was in, the life-threatening danger, pushed Mark onward and he stepped up to tap on the driver's window.

The driver started and snapped his head around, eyes wide, mouth an O of surprise. Confusion and fear mingled on his face for a moment, but he started the engine and lowered the window a few inches.

"Can I help you?"

"I need your car."

"What? I don't understand—"

Mark interrupted him. "I need your car. It's life-or-death."

Silence, punctuated by an expression of surprised disbelief on the driver's face. "I'm not giving you my car, douche bag. Fuck off."

Mark pulled the gun from his jacket and pointed it at the driver, painfully aware of just how far off from his core values he'd strayed. But, he told himself, this was all for the greater good. This was to save Pearce—*Aaron, his name was Aaron*—and to stop the terrorists' murderous plan. A simple carjacking was worth it for all that, wasn't it? "I need your car. Now."

The driver held his hands up and widened his eyes. "Are you crazy? Holy fucking shit. Are you carjacking me?"

"Get out." Mark stepped back from the car and looked around furtively, hoping no witnesses were around. "Now. Come on, get out."

The man fumbled the door open and stepped out onto the icy asphalt, hands still held up. "Okay. I'm out, I'm out. Don't shoot me, dude."

"Just stay cool and you won't get hurt, okay?" Mark slid into the seat, still warm from the driver's ass. He put the gun on the passenger seat and shifted into reverse, then thought for a second and said through the window, "Look, I'm sorry about all this. I'll take care of your car, I just… I just need it right now. It's life or death. Sorry."

The driver's face clouded with anger and he lowered his hands. "You're sorry? You're stealing my car! I just bought it."

"I really don't think you "just bought it," did you?" Mark asked. "It's at least four years old. I'll take care of it, don't worry." He backed out of the space, then hit the brakes when the driver shouted after him, "I'm calling the cops!"

Mark put the car in park and got out, one foot on the asphalt, and pointed the gun over the roof of the car. "You can't do that."

The driver's hands went up again. "Okay, I was kidding. Really, it was a joke. No cops. I promise."

Mark weighed his options. He could feel the van with Pearce inside getting farther and farther away. But he couldn't risk getting the cops involved, either. He didn't know whom to trust, but he knew he had to act fast or lose Pearce forever. "Get in."

"What?"

"Get in the fucking car!" Mark shouted. "Now! Right fucking now!"

The driver ran to the passenger door and scrambled into the car, hands held up. "Okay, I'm in the car. Oh shit, I'm in, I'm in. Be cool, man. Be cool."

Mark hit the button for the gate and shifted the car into drive. "Buckle up," he said. "We're going to be moving fast."

He put the gun in the netted compartment in the driver's door, away from the driver's reach, and pulled out into the street. The tires slid across the icy surface and Mark struggled with the wheel, afraid for a moment this whole insane idea would end with him ramming the stolen car into the front of Phong's Garden. But then the tires found purchase, and the car shot down the street. He ran red lights as the driver hyperventilated beside him, hands gripping the handle above his door, eyes wide and staring straight ahead.

"What's your name?" Mark asked.

"W-What?" the driver stammered.

"What's your name?" Mark repeated.

"Andy."

"Okay, Andy, my name's Mark, all right? I'm not going to hurt you."

"Okay."

"There's some trouble going down and I really needed a car, and you just happened to pull in at the right moment, I'm sorry."

"Yeah, okay." Andy flinched as Mark ran a red light. "Be careful, okay? I just … Just be careful, please."

"I need to move fast, Andy," Mark said, his head swiveling back and forth at cross streets as he looked for the white van. "I wasted a lot of time arguing with you, and I lost sight of them."

"Who?"

"A white-panel van. Help me look for it."

"White-panel van?" Andy looked down side streets and at the road ahead of them, still hanging on to the handle. "What kind? Ford? GM?"

"I don't know, they all look alike. Just look for a white van. The right taillight is burned out." Mark was running out of road and in another few streets would need to turn right or left at Atwater Street or else drive into the Detroit River. "Fuck, I can't lose them."

"What kind of trouble is this?" Andy asked, trying to keep his voice even, but the fear he felt was clear in the tremble. "Someone you're dating? Is she with someone else?"

Mark shook his head. "It's not like that, Andy. It's more serious. Much more serious. Just help me look for the van."

They didn't see it until Mark came to a stop at Atwater; Andy pointed out his window and shouted, "There! I see a white van! Right there!"

Mark turned right and weaved in and out of traffic until he was three car lengths behind the van. The van stopped for a traffic light, and when he saw that the right taillight was burned out, he felt relief flood his system. It was the right van, he was sure of it. And really, how many white-panel vans were driving around downtown Detroit, anyway?

"Is that them?" Andy asked. He had released his hold on the handle above him and sat forward in the seat, staring at the van. Andy seemed to be getting into the game now that Mark had put the gun away and they had found the van.

"Yeah, it looks like it." Mark said. "The right taillight is burned out. I'm pretty sure it's them."

Mark caught slow movement from the corner of his eye and turned his head to see Andy reaching for the door handle.

"Don't even think about it," Mark growled. "You're staying with me, got it?"

"What are you going to do?" Andy asked, trying for bravery. "Shoot me in the back as I run from my own car?"

"If I have to," Mark told him and held his gaze until Andy dropped his eyes and put his hands in his lap. "Thank you." The light changed, and he followed the van through the multiple landscapes of Detroit: the burned-out husks of abandoned homes, revived shopping centers and town houses, the shuttered doors and shattered windows of vacant factories. As other traffic thinned out, Mark eased up on the accelerator and fell farther behind the van to keep from being spotted.

Andy passed the time staring silently out the window, hands fisted in his lap. After a long interval of silence, Mark felt the man deserved some kind of explanation and cleared his throat. "Look, Andy, I'm sorry about all this. I got mixed up in something kind of dangerous, and I went to the FBI about it, and well, things got complicated."

Andy turned to face him. "Bullshit."

Mark shook his head. "I swear to God it's not. The man in that van up there is an FBI agent and he was protecting me from a terrorist group because I overheard their plans to blow something up."

"Jesus." Andy looked down at his hands. "What were they going to blow up?"

Mark shrugged. "I couldn't figure that out. They were talking about blast radius and viscosity and a scheduled departure on Valentine's Day."

"Valentine's Day?" Andy said. "That's in two days."

"I know," Mark replied. "So we're kind of under a time crunch to understand it."

Andy was silent again, then asked, "So if he was protecting you, what happened?"

Mark sighed. "I don't know, really. He went out to get dinner and when he came back someone was with him. There was a spy in the FBI office here in Detroit, someone working with the terrorist cell, and my identity was compromised. We had to go into hiding and didn't have a lot of money. We've been staying in your building, in a loft on the third floor. A friend of mine lives there and I knew he'd be out of town on business so I suggested we stay there." Mark turned to look at Andy's profile in the glow of the dashboard. "I'm sorry I stole your car—"

"And held a gun on me," Andy added.

Mark nodded. "And held a gun on you. But I'm desperate."

Andy pointed ahead and said, "Hey, they're stopping at that old house."

Mark eased the car to the curb and switched off the lights and engine. Turning to look at Andy, Mark said, "I'm not crazy, all right? And I'm not going to hurt you. Just don't get out in this neighborhood, please."

"Don't worry," Andy said, looking around at the looming skeletons of burned-out and deserted houses. "I think staying in here with a crazy guy who broke into a friend's loft and carries a gun is safer than being out there."

The van pulled into the rutted dirt drive of a house standing all alone in the middle of a block that had, at one time, probably been a thriving community. Now just husks of homes stood interspersed between crumbling foundations to mark the spots where families had once been raised. The van stopped partway up the drive, and they watched two men get out. One of the men reached back in and jerked another out of the back. Even from this distance, Mark could tell it was Pearce, and he drew in a breath. Andy watched his reaction carefully and asked, "Are you involved with this agent?"

"It's complicated," Mark replied.

"You keep saying that," Andy said.

"Because it's true," Mark snapped. "Give me a minute to think about what to do."

The van pulled farther up the drive and disappeared behind the house as the three men climbed steps to the front door and went inside.

Andy cleared his throat and asked, "Not to, like, mention the obvious, but why not call the cops?"

Mark shook his head. "Too risky. There might be someone working with them at the police who could tip them off."

"Jesus, really?"

"Really."

"Any ideas then?" Andy asked.

"Not really." Mark picked up the gun and switched off the safety, then chambered a round, noticing that Andy leaned away from him against the passenger door. "But I'm going out there."

"Mark, this is crazy," Andy told him. "There's just you against at least three of them. And they're killers, right? You said so yourself, they're planning a terrorist strike in a few days."

Mark took a breath and tried to keep his stomach settled. "I know. But I've got to do something."

Andy watched him a moment. "He means this much to you?"

Mark looked at Andy and nodded solemnly. "He does."

Rolling his eyes, Andy threw his hands up in the air. "I'm going to fucking regret this, but... How can I help you?"

"You don't have to do this, Andy. Really, you've done enough already." Mark looked out the windshield and saw the van's driver bound up the front steps, turning to point the remote back at the vehicle. They heard the beep of the van's alarm being set before the man entered the house. Mark pressed his lips together in a tight smile. "But if you really wanted to help, I just came up with an idea."

He saw Andy swallow hard and look out the windshield at the dark house up the block, conflicting emotions playing over his face. "Okay," Andy said. "A couple years ago I dated a guy who made me feel the way you do. I let him get away, and I still regret it." He took a breath and nodded. "What's the plan?"

CHAPTER 11

Pearce sat in a rickety wooden chair, hands duct taped together behind the straight back, ankles taped to the chair legs. They were in the kitchen of an abandoned house: rotting cupboards lined the walls, and he could hear the scratch-and-scurry sounds of rats inside the walls and cabinets. Black trash bags covered the windows, blocking all views into the house and keeping the weak battery-powered lantern light from attracting attention. He could hear voices in the next room, Morgan mostly, giving orders.

Twisting his wrists, Pearce tried to loosen the tape keeping him in the chair, but Morgan had made sure he wasn't going anywhere. With a sigh, Pearce gave up and closed his eyes, thinking about Mark, hoping he was safe. He couldn't help feeling like he had failed in his assignment to keep Mark secure until the trial, and he feared he would never see Mark again. An icy emptiness opened in his chest at this last thought, and he tried hard to conjure up the memory of Mark's face in profile as he slept, but at the moment he couldn't do it. All he could see was a vision of Mark screaming in pain and terror. It wasn't supposed to end this way. They were the good guys; they were supposed to win.

"Taking a nap?"

Pearce opened his eyes and glared across the room at Morgan. "Just thinking about the best way to kill you."

Morgan chuckled and shook his head. "Same old Aaron, dramatic to the last."

"Fuck you, Morgan."

"We tried that before," Morgan said and stepped up to tower over him. "For some reason, we didn't seem to take." Morgan ran a hand along his cheek, and Pearce jerked his head away. "Oh my, aren't we touchy?"

"What do you want with me?" Pearce said. "If you're going to kill me, just get it over with, okay? Stop playing your usual games."

Morgan stepped across the room, taking off his suit jacket to expose his shoulder holster and weapon. He stopped in front of the sink and looked down into it as he rolled up his sleeves. "It's a shame you feel that way, Aaron. We could have had some fun together, for old time's sake."

"You were a lousy lay back then," Pearce said with a sneer. "I doubt you've let your ego relax enough to improve."

Morgan smiled and shook his head; then, moving faster than Pearce would have given him credit for, the man snatched a small knife from the sink and knelt beside him. The knife rested just beneath Pearce's left eye, the point not quite breaking the skin. Pearce sucked in a breath and held very still, his eye rolling to see Morgan's face.

"Your attitude is"—Morgan paused to consider word options —"disappointing. I was hoping we could catch up a little, maybe have a beer or two, relieve some tension together. But..." Morgan applied more pressure to the knife and Pearce closed his eyes, waiting for the flash of pain and wet *pop* of his eye coming out. "You don't appear to be receptive to that. So, on with business it is."

The knife was removed from his face, and Pearce opened his eyes, blinking back tears and looking around for Morgan's position. A blur of motion from his right followed by the sharp pain of the knife sinking into the hollow of that shoulder caused Pearce to throw back his head and scream. Pain exploded in his shoulder and ratcheted through his body. Pearce clenched his fists as his body spasmed, pain shooting up and down his right arm, the chair creaking beneath him. He struggled to remain conscious, taking breaths and diverting his attention from the wound. Cold sweat popped out on his forehead and ran down his face as his stomach turned dangerously close to nausea. From the corner of his eye, Pearce saw Morgan step around from behind him, casually looking at the hilt of the knife protruding from Pearce's shoulder.

"Ah, now that's a shame," Morgan said and made *tsking* sounds as he shook his head. "That looks like it hurts. Not life threatening—well, not yet anyway—but enough to screw up your aim for sure. Too bad, and you were such a good shot, too."

Pearce groaned and leaned forward, breathing deeply and keeping his eyes away from the sight of the knife in his shoulder. He willed himself to remain conscious and raised his head to glare at Morgan.

"Now, let's talk about Mark Beecher," Morgan said and

returned to the sink. "Where would he go now that he's, shall we say, out from under you, hmm?"

"Hell, maybe," Pearce growled. "Why don't you go there and check?"

Morgan let out a humorless bark of a laugh. "Funny, actually, because there is a city in Michigan named Hell. Not the first place I would think of, but I'll send someone through it just to be sure." He turned away from the sink with another, longer knife in hand. The weak light of the lantern glinted dully off the blade, reminding Pearce of jack-o'-lanterns on Halloween. He closed his eyes and turned his head away.

"One more time, Aaron," Morgan said and stood in front of Pearce. "Where is Mark Beecher?"

Pearce raised his head and looked him in the eye. No words were necessary; Morgan could tell what he was thinking and let out his breath with a sigh.

"So be it." Morgan raised the knife. "Sad, really, because this one's going lower, and you did so love to jog."

A car alarm blared into life from just outside the back door of the house. Morgan faltered, lowering the knife to his side and turning his head to look toward the sound. The two camouflaged goons appeared in a doorway, eyes alert, guns ready.

Morgan looked at them in silence for a moment, then waved a hand toward the sound. "Well, go check it out!"

The men nearly ran into each other to get to the front door, and Morgan looked down at Pearce with a shake of his head. "Hickam did not recruit from the smartest of gene pools, as you can probably tell." He juggled the knife a moment, then stabbed it down hard into the seat of the chair between Pearce's legs.

Pearce jumped and heard the chair bottom split before Morgan turned to stomp off through the house.

Pearce took slow, deep breaths and shifted his position on the chair, gasping at the hot spark of pain in his shoulder. The seat beneath him split a little more and the knife stuck in the wood leaned away from him. He took more deep breaths and clenched his fists, straining his arms as he channeled the pain in his shoulder into anger, and from that into strength. He pushed backward until the chair back let go its tenuous hold on the seat with a hearty *crack!* nearly toppling him onto his back. He scooted around on the broken seat until it too split and the knife Morgan had stuck into the chair dropped to the floor. Pearce fell to the floor on his back, hands still taped to the seat back trapped beneath him, and stifled a cry of pain as the fall jostled his shoulder. He rolled to his side to relieve pressure on his arms and gasped as the knife in his shoulder bumped a chair leg. Pearce swooned and nearly blacked out, but instead he closed his eyes and held his breath until the feeling passed.

Rolling onto his side, Pearce scooted himself across the remnants of the chair until his bound hands touched the handle of the knife that had split the seat. Sweat rolled down his face and into his eyes as he fumbled to hold the knife at the right angle to cut the tape. He felt the blade touch the tape and began to saw awkwardly at his bindings, gasping at the flares of pain the motion caused in his shoulder.

Outside, the car alarm stopped, leaving a sudden, deadly silence in its wake.

CHAPTER 12

Mark literally did not know what to do next. Andy had set off the alarm on the van as planned, and now Mark watched from behind a tree as the two camo-garbed goons left the porch and headed for the back, guns in hand. He had planned it all up to this point, the car alarm attracting their attention and the lackeys coming out to investigate. But now he had to think of the next step, and the only thing left was to go inside the house.

He stayed low and ran across the barren yard, quietly climbing the steps and entering the house, the gun at his side and his heart in his throat. He heard a crash from down the hall toward the back of the house, and someone let out a scream of pain, someone who sounded an awful lot like Pearce. His stomach twisted at the thought of Pearce in pain, and he fought back tears, focusing on what lay before him. A closed door stood at the end of the hall, one of those swinging doors that usually led to a kitchen.

Moving as quietly as possible, Mark made his way down the

hall, gun held in both hands like Pearce had shown him. It was heavy and shook in his grip, but he couldn't tell if the shaking was from the weight or fear. He could hear Pearce's words, almost feel his warm breath in his ear again as he gave instructions: *"You need to relax. It will have some kick when you fire, so don't lock your elbows."*

Dark shadows crouched in the hallway before him, and two doors opened on dark rooms beyond. He stopped just shy of the first room to gather his courage, glanced behind him, out the open front door to the hulks of abandoned homes across the street. Turning toward the door at the end of the hall, he took a breath and forced himself to take a step closer. He moved past the first dark doorway and realized his mistake just a moment too late as an arm snaked out of the shadows and wrapped around his neck. He was pulled back against a man's firm chest, and a gun jabbed into his side.

"Well, well, well," a deep voice hissed in his ear. "Look who's come for dinner."

Mark started to struggle, but the man pushed the gun harder into his side. "Don't make me kill you right away, as a favor to me, okay? I want Pearce to watch you die. Now drop the gun. Go ahead, just release it."

Mark blinked back tears as he let the gun fall from his hand. The weapon hit the floor with a heavy *thump*, and the gun in his side pulled away as the man crouched down to pick it up. Without a thought, Mark ran forward and pushed through the swinging door to the kitchen. He heard the man curse behind him as he quickly surveyed the room: dirty, broken cabinets; filthy linoleum floor; covered windows. A chair lay broken on the floor, blood smeared across the dirty tiles. His stomach knotted at the sight of the blood, knowing it was Pearce's, and hoped he wasn't too late, that they hadn't already killed him. He wanted to live at least long enough to see Pearce's brown eyes one more time.

The sound of footsteps behind him pulled Mark back to his situation, and he pressed his back against the wall, one hand holding the door open. As the footsteps closed in on the doorway, Mark braced himself against the wall and pushed the door back on the double hinge, feeling the satisfying thump and tremble of contact with his pursuer.

A vicious curse sounded, and then a solid kick pushed the door back to him, forcing him to take two steps into the kitchen. The man held the door open with one hand, and a gun on him with the other. Blood streamed from his nose down over his lips and chin, and his eyes glittered with a cold fury that Mark could see even in the dimly lit room.

"You're quite the little bitch, aren't you?" The man turned his head to call over his shoulder. "Bill! Lonnie!"

Mark swallowed hard, thinking of Andy out in the frozen yard. Mark hoped he was all right; he had been unlucky enough to be in the wrong place at the wrong time, but he had stepped up to help him out when he didn't have to.

The man before him—it must be Morgan—furrowed his brow and tried again. "Bill! Lonnie! Get your fucking asses in here!"

Mark took a step back, his foot coming to rest on a piece of the broken chair. He glanced down and saw that he was standing on the splintered end of a chair rail. Carefully watching Morgan, Mark eased back another step. There was an open doorway leading to another room behind him and to his left.

"Stop moving!" Morgan shouted at him, and Mark froze in place. "Who was outside with you?"

"The police," Mark said, his voice cracking.

"That's a lie. I would have heard about that." Morgan held the kitchen door open with his foot and shot a look over his shoulder.

Mark saw his chance and crouched, picking up the splintered chair rail and rushing forward. He drove the jagged end of the chair rail into Morgan's gut. As the wood pierced the man's skin, Morgan fired a shot, and Mark felt the heat of the gunpowder and the wind of the bullet an inch from his cheek. Morgan fell back into the hallway and Mark ran to the other doorway, diving through it to the room beyond.

CHAPTER 13

Pearce was about to round the corner from the trash-strewn living room to the entrance foyer when he heard the gunshot followed by the sound of someone hitting the floor behind him. Turning, Pearce held the knife in his left hand and crouched down, his right arm hanging loose at his side as he crept through the shadows to peer around the doorway into what used to be a dining room. A shadow moved, and he tensed, then blinked in surprise. Mark hurried through the shadows toward him, head turned away to look over his shoulder. Pearce's heart soared at the sight of Mark, even as he mentally cursed him for putting himself in danger to rescue him, and at that moment he knew he was in love. Mark was walking into a trap, though. He didn't know the house was laid out in a circle, but Morgan did, and now Pearce did too.

Pearce heard Morgan's footsteps approaching the living room from the front of the house and did the only thing that came to mind. Standing up and holding the knife in his weak right hand against his leg and out of the way, he grabbed Mark as the man ran past him and pulled him down to the floor with him, grimacing at the pain in his shoulder.

"It's Pearce," he whispered as Mark struggled beneath him. At his words, Mark went still, and Pearce felt Mark's hand grip his shoulder tight. He gasped. Darkness swam up to engulf him, but he shook it off. "Careful, I'm hurt."

"Oh God," Mark said. "I'm sorry." He kissed him quickly and said, "I thought you were dead."

"And I thought you were safe," Pearce replied, then kissed him again. "What the fuck are you doing here?"

"I couldn't let them kill you," Mark whispered. "I had to try and save you."

"Dammit, Mark, that wasn't the plan," Pearce hissed.

"I don't care about the plan," Mark said, eyes glittering with defiance in the weak glow of the lanterns. "I care about you."

Pearce kissed him, hard, then said, "Stay with me."

"I will," Mark replied, and in his response, Pearce heard his commitment.

A footstep sounded from the hallway, and they fell silent.

Mark whispered, "He's got your gun. I stabbed him, but he's got two guns."

"He's coming from the front of the house," Pearce whispered back and turned his head, watching the doorway carefully. A shadow moved, and he squinted, waiting for the perfect moment. Finally, Morgan stepped into the living room, and Pearce rolled over, cocking his left arm back, holding the knife and his breath as he forced himself to wait. Morgan did not see them in the far corner, as he was looking into the shadows closer to where he stood, his hand over the wound in his stomach. Pearce counted to ten, then threw the knife. It hit Morgan high in the chest with a solid, wet *thwack*, and the man cried out and staggered back into the shadows.

Pearce grabbed Mark's hand and got to his feet. "Come on."

They advanced carefully to the hall doorway, and Pearce moved fast around the corner. The blast of a gunshot made them both jump and plaster dust coated them as the bullet hit the wall a foot away.

"Get outside!" Pearce shoved Mark out the front door and staggered after him.

"This way!" Mark grabbed Pearce's hand and pulled him to the sidewalk and down the street. Behind them, another gunshot made them duck, but it went wide.

A car down the block flicked its headlights on and off, and Mark ran toward it. As Mark jumped in the front, Pearce fell into the backseat, lying down and holding his right arm as still as possible. The driver peeled out, and as they passed the house, Pearce heard a volley of gunshots. Two of the shots hit the back quarter panel, and the driver cursed.

"Are you okay?" Mark asked, leaning around the seat to look back at him. Pearce had just enough strength to nod up at him before he closed his eyes and drifted away.

———

WHEN PEARCE CAME TO, he was in a hospital bed with an IV line in his arm. His right arm lay in a sling across his chest, and his shoulder throbbed. A metallic taste coated his mouth, and he licked his dry lips as he turned his head to look around the room.

Mark was slouched in a chair in the corner, fast asleep, his face pale, clothes a mess.

"Hey," Pearce said, his voice raspy. "Mark."

Mark stirred and blinked, then jumped to his feet and approached the bed.

"Hey, hi there," Mark said, stroking the side of his face. "How are you?"

"Thirsty," Pearce croaked. Mark held up a Styrofoam cup of water with a straw, and Pearce sipped gratefully. "Thanks." He looked at Mark's handsome face, his eyes ringed with shadows of exhaustion, his jaw covered with a couple of days' growth of dark blond beard. "You doing okay? You hurt?"

Mark shook his head and smiled at him. "I'm tired, but I'm not hurt."

Pearce nodded, then narrowed his eyes. "You took a big risk coming after me."

Mark shrugged. "Yeah, and?"

Pearce shook his head and turned his face away to hide his grin. Mark, stubborn to the last. He would probably argue with the grim reaper as he lay on his deathbed. Pearce wondered how Mark would look as he aged, then surprised himself by hoping he would be around to see for himself. With a breath, Pearce nodded to his right arm, then looked back at Mark's face. "How bad is my shoulder?"

"You're okay," Mark told him. "The doctors said you'll be all right after some physical therapy."

"Well, there's that to look forward to." They both laughed a little; then Pearce frowned at him. "How did we get here?"

"After you and I got out of the house, Andy drove us here to

Harper Hospital, and I talked with the police while you were in surgery. Agent Bata has been here as well."

Pearce frowned up at him. "Andy?"

Mark smiled and nodded. "Yeah. After they drove off with you, I carjacked a guy who pulled into the parking lot. He really stepped up and he didn't have to. He set off the alarm on their van, then used some old branch in the yard to clock the two guys Morgan had working with him. We owe him a lot. Morgan got away, but Bata has an APB out on him. They don't think he'll get far, especially with two stab wounds."

"Jesus, how long have I been out?" Pearce asked.

"About two and a half days." Mark took his left hand and squeezed it. "One more piece of news: they figured out what the Kings of Rebellion were targeting."

Pearce raised his eyebrows. "They did? What was it?"

"The Detroit Princess, a riverboat that makes a loop on the Detroit River. Apparently they're having a cruise on Valentine's Day, and the plan was to fill the engine room with explosives."

Pearce frowned. "That's pretty bad, but how come in your notes on their conversations, the casualty rate was expected to be in the hundreds or possibly thousands? A riverboat isn't that big."

"Well, the boat happens to pass over the tunnel beneath the river that connects Detroit and Windsor, Canada. A lot of people use the tunnel rather than the Ambassador Bridge to commute between the US and Canada. They were trying not just to blow up the riverboat but hopefully flood the tunnel as well."

Pearce nodded. "That explains the comments about viscosity and blast radius."

"Yep. They were trying to figure out how much the river water would lessen the impact of the explosion."

Pearce's mouth went dry at the thought of how close they'd come to succeeding. "That's fucked up."

Mark nodded. "More than fucked up. And there's more good news. They found out a maintenance guy on the riverboat was a member of the Kings of Rebellion. They arrested him at work this morning, and when they went to search his apartment, they found Harold Hickam sleeping on his couch."

"They caught Hickam?" Pearce barked a hoarse laugh. "Sleeping on his lackey's couch?"

Mark laughed as well. "Yep. Can you believe it?"

Pearce shook his head, then looked up at Mark. "Well, I guess that's it, then. The bad guys are caught and you're safe."

"Well, Morgan's still out there, but yeah." Mark pressed his lips together and nodded. "I guess that's it."

Silence filled the room, and Pearce felt something cold burning in his chest. It wasn't pain from his shoulder or the medication; it was the thought of going back to Washington, DC alone and leaving Mark behind.

"Look," he said, "I'm no good at relationships. Never have been. But I'm going to need to rest up while my shoulder heals, and that's going to give me a lot of free time." Pearce grinned. "I'm also not good with free time, if you can believe it."

Mark gave him an exaggerated look of disbelief. "No, really? Don't forget, I was holed up in a loft apartment with you for almost a week. I believe it."

"Anyway," Pearce said with a mock scowl. "What I was wondering is...if you would be at all interested in, well, maybe coming to visit me in DC?"

Mark's eyes widened, and the subsequent smile lit up his face so much, Pearce felt it warm the cold spot inside his chest.

"Are you sure?" Mark said. "I mean, you don't have to do this just because I risked my life to save yours."

Pearce grinned and shook his head. "Well, we can discuss that during your visit. And you can demonstrate your prowess as a station chef. I expect to sample all items from your repertoire."

Mark leaned down and kissed him softly on the mouth, his tongue flickering with promise across Pearce's lips. "You can try every single one of the items in my repertoire…Aaron."

Pearce rolled his eyes, grinning with embarrassed satisfaction. "Yeah, yeah, you found out my first name."

"I like it," Mark said as he sat on the edge of the bed, grabbing Pearce's left hand and holding it tight. "It fits. But it's going to take me some time to get out of the habit of calling you Pearce."

Pearce didn't say anything. He just lay looking up at Mark, promising himself that this relationship was going to be different. This one would last long enough for him to hear Mark get comfortable calling him Aaron.

SHACKED UP

Keep reading for a preview of *Shacked Up*,
book two in the Up to Trouble series.

SHACKED UP
CHAPTER ONE

Another glance into the rearview mirror made Mark certain he was being followed.

The red Escort had been two cars behind him ever since he left Pearce's apartment. Always two cars, never more and never less. Just like Morgan would have learned in FBI training.

Mark turned his attention to the stoplight before him. He needed to stay calm and think; that was his priority. He had known the day would come when Morgan would show up again, but Mark had thought he and Pearce might have had a little more time.

The light changed, and Mark burned rubber as he sped through the intersection. He shifted his gaze from the street in front of him to the rearview mirror, watching with satisfaction as the red Escort became mired behind a city bus and a minivan.

He took the next right, then made another right and back-tracked a few blocks, turning right again. He came to a stop at a red light on the street he had just left. If his calculations were correct, he was now behind the red Escort, driven, perhaps, by Robert Morgan, the traitor FBI agent who had tried to kill them both back in Detroit. Now was his chance to find out for sure. He should be able to move up alongside the Escort and get a look at the driver.

As he waited for the light to change, Mark picked up his cell phone and dialed Pearce's number. Now that he had seen the Escort a third time, he needed to tell Pearce.

"Hey." Pearce's voice, gruff as usual, was also tainted with boredom. He was stuck behind a desk—light duty, they called it —compiling database search requests sent to him from agents in the field during his recuperation from injuries sustained on the job. Despite the tension of Mark's situation, the sound of Pearce's voice brought to mind thoughts of the man, and Mark could see Pearce as clearly as if he were sitting in the seat next to him: short-cut brown hair, normally alert brown eyes heavy with boredom, his six-foot-four, muscular frame cramped at his desk. The image sent a shock of lust right to his crotch, as usual.

"Hey." Mark cleared his throat, made himself focus on the issue at hand. "Um, so… Have you noticed anyone following you to work lately?"

"What do you mean?" Pearce asked, his tone sharpening immediately, FBI instincts kicking in. "You all right?"

Before Mark could answer, the driver behind him honked the horn. The light had turned green.

"Sorry!" Mark lifted a hand to the driver in apology and turned the corner, the phone still held to his ear.

"Mark?" Pearce demanded answers and assurance, just like normal. It was just another day here in Washington, DC; things were going to be okay. "What's going on? Are you okay?"

"I'm fine. I'm okay. I just…" Mark maneuvered his way through traffic, paying only half attention to what he was saying to Pearce.

"Goddammit, Mark," Pearce snapped. "Stop talking while you're driving. It's dangerous and illegal here. Pull over and tell me what's going on."

Mark grunted, his gaze bouncing between cars lined up in front of him, searching for the red Escort. It was nowhere in sight, and something tightened inside his chest, threatening his ability to breathe. Before, when he had seen the Escort behind him, he'd been scared, but at least he had known where the threat lay. Now he had no idea of the car's location, and that, it turned out, was much worse.

"Mark!"

The angry tone made Mark jump, and he said, "Okay, okay, I'm pulling over. Hold on."

Mark pulled off the main road onto a side street, then into the tiny parking lot of a group of town houses. He turned into an empty space reserved for town house 101A and put his car in Park. He kept his gaze on the driveway, alert for a glimpse of the red car.

"All right, I'm parked."

"Good," Pearce said. "Now, what the hell is going on?"

Mark told him about the red Escort, how it had shown up for a third time, two cars behind him, just like before. "It's a classic tail. Always two cars back."

"Is it a bright red car?" Pearce asked.

Mark frowned. "Yeah, a brighter shade."

"Odd choice of color to use if you're going to follow someone," Pearce said.

"Oh, yeah." Mark nodded. "Good point. So you don't think it's him?"

"I didn't say that," Pearce replied. "Did you see the driver?"

"No."

"Did he make any threatening moves? Try to hit you or run you off the road?"

Mark's stomach clenched at the thought, but he forced himself to reply in as calm a voice as he could manage. "No. Nothing like that. It just… The car followed me from about a block away from the apartment to probably a block before I got to work."

"But you haven't seen the driver?"

"No, but it feels like a tail, you know?" Mark heard the defensiveness in his tone and immediately wished he could take the words back.

"Hey, I'm not trying to make you feel like you've done something wrong," Pearce said, his voice softening. "I'm just asking questions, okay?"

Mark nodded and closed his eyes. "Okay. Sorry."

"No need to apologize. I'm glad you're alert and able to recognize potential threats."

The laugh slipped out before Mark knew it. "Great. So this is what my day will be like from now on? Do I need an armed escort to drive to work?"

Work. Mark glanced at the clock in the dash and swore.

"What? What's wrong?" Pearce asked, alarmed again at Mark's swearing.

"It's late. I'm late. I've gotta go."

"Oh, yeah, it is late," Pearce said. "Sure you're okay to drive?"

A quiet, confusing mixture of relief and mild resentment

warred within Mark. Pearce cared about him—Mark knew that, could tell not just from the tone of the man's voice, but from the way he had treated him the last four months they had been living together. Sometimes, though, Mark wondered if Pearce still felt like he was on the job, that he needed to protect Mark because his assignment wasn't complete, since Robert Morgan had escaped. When he had those thoughts, however, Mark tried to remind himself about the little things Pearce did to show how much he cared: the spooning at night, the coffee in the morning, made how Mark liked it, the new pots and pans so Mark could work on new recipe ideas. There was genuine affection between them, but Mark didn't want to have to keep running to Pearce every time he was scared of something or someone. He needed to find a way to get back the independence he had had in Detroit, before Pearce had stormed into his life. He needed to find a way to be himself and still be with Pearce, or this relationship wasn't going to work out at all.

Too much to think about now, when he was running late for work. But definitely something Mark had to figure out—and soon.

"Yeah," Mark assured him. "I'm okay to drive, thanks. I'll talk to you later."

"Be careful," Pearce said. "And no talking on the phone while driving. It would look bad for my clean-cut image here if my boyfriend were ticketed for illegal cell phone use."

Mark was surprised by his own chuckle. "Oh, well, we can't have that, now, can we, Agent Pearce?"

"No, we can't." Pearce's tone shifted back to serious. "Do you want me to come there and follow you to work?"

Mark shook his head, then remembered Pearce couldn't see

him. "No. I'll be okay. If I see the car again, I'll turn into a police station or something right away."

"Good." Pearce hesitated. "Well, talk to you later."

"Yeah. Bye."

Mark disconnected the call and sat a moment, staring at the brick wall in front of him. Sometimes he was amazed at the swerve his life had taken. Four months after meeting Pearce in Detroit, Mark had moved to Washington, DC—and into Pearce's apartment. A pretty quick change in living arrangements, by anyone's standards.

And now he was going to be really late for work.

Mark backed out of the parking space, then pulled onto the street. He sat at the red light at the intersection, watching his rearview mirror for the red Escort as he waited for the light to turn green.

By the time he reached the small brick building that housed the office and kitchen of Filibuster Catering, Mark had not seen the suspicious car again. He parked in the lot behind the building, took a moment to gather his thoughts, and pushed the idea of pursuit out of his mind. He had only had this job as catering assistant two weeks, and it needed his full attention.

He got out of his car and let himself into the catering kitchen through the heavy back door. A long, dimly lit hallway opened to a wide kitchen with two prep islands, two ovens and sets of burners, three sinks, two dishwashers, and two large refrigerators.

Audra Hodgson, the owner of Filibuster Catering, stood at one of the prep islands, cleaning mushroom caps. She was in her late sixties, with cool, hazel eyes and softly styled silver hair worn shoulder length. The other two employees, Darlene and

Brenda, stood across the island from Audra, both busy chopping and mixing ingredients. All three women looked up when Mark rounded the corner from the hallway.

Audra cocked an expertly threaded silver eyebrow. "Traffic bad?"

Mark turned away to hang up his jacket and grab his chef whites. "I had to take a little detour to get around some backups."

"This isn't going to become a habit, is it?" Audra asked.

Mark turned to look at her and shook his head. "No, it won't."

"Good. I hired you to take some of the load off Darlene and Brenda and me. I need to know you're a team player." Audra raised both eyebrows this time. "Are you a team player, Mark?"

"I am," Mark said. "I'll be sure to be on time from now on."

Audra nodded once and tipped her head toward the refrigerator. "We've got a party this evening. Darlene and I will continue to work on the appetizers. I need you and Brenda to check the chicken in the marinade and then prep the potatoes and vegetables that we'll steam at the house."

A thread of disappointment stitched through Mark's gut. "There's a party tonight?"

Brenda ducked her head, hiding a smirk as a ginger-colored curl bounced alongside her face. Audra, however, was not smiling as she shot him a sharp look. "We've discussed this, Mark. Several times."

Mark blushed and dropped his gaze. "Sorry. You're right. I just... I just forgot what day it was today. I knew about the party, just got messed up on the day, that's all."

"We prepped the chicken all afternoon yesterday." Audra obviously wasn't ready to let his memory lapse go.

Mark pressed his lips tight before saying, "I know. I'm sorry. I'm here and in the moment." He let out a breath and shook his hands to release tension. "So. A party tonight."

Audra looked down at the mushroom caps again. "Yes. Senator Baxter's assistant is having a dinner party." Audra grinned as she swept the mushroom caps into a bowl. "I've been running this business for six years and have just this year started booking the higher-tier parties."

"A senator's assistant is higher tier?" Darlene asked. She was a short woman with wire-frame glasses and soft, rounded cheeks. She had worked for Audra just over two years and usually helped in the kitchen only during the day, prepping for parties, as she was a single mother with a young daughter.

"Absolutely, Darlene," Audra said. "Who does the senator ask to set up his luncheons or small gatherings?"

Brenda leaned in close to Darlene and whispered, "His assistant."

Darlene scowled at Brenda, then turned back to Audra. "Well, yeah, I knew that. But how many catered parties does a senator throw without his wife getting involved?"

Audra lifted one corner of her mouth in a small, private smile. "Oh, dear Darlene, you'd be surprised."

Brenda laughed and turned to the sink to wash her hands. "Come on, Mark. Let's get to work."

"Yeah, sure," Mark said and followed Brenda across the room, mentally chastising himself for forgetting about the dinner party tonight. Later he would text Pearce and let him know, but Mark had really wanted to be home that evening; he felt that he and Pearce needed to talk about this red Escort some more.

As Mark trimmed broccoli spears beside Brenda, he fell into the comfortable rhythm of chopping and allowed his mind to stray back to Detroit. He thought about the moment he had met Pearce in the FBI office, the gut-punch feeling of attraction at their introduction, the terror that mixed with it when they were shot at in an alley before holing up in the vacant loft apartment of Mark's ex-boyfriend, Eric.

The sexual tension between them had been thick—even on that first day—and when they had finally succumbed to their attraction, Mark had felt something inside him loosen. He had known after that first night together that he was in love with Pearce. But now, months later, when Mark went back to Pearce's apartment every night to have dinner with the man, watch TV, and share his bed, he could not bring himself to say it to Pearce. No, that would never do. Pearce was going to have to say it first. Mark knew the type of man he had become involved with: Pearce was a heartbreaker, a lover but not an in-lover. Pearce was steady sex and, occasionally, reluctantly romantic. The man had built dozens of walls around his innermost spaces, and even though Pearce had asked Mark to stay with him in Washington, DC while he had gone through rehab for his wounds, and after that, move in with him, Mark knew he had a ways to go before he would get to know the true man that lay within Aaron Pearce. He had to be patient. If Mark tried to force Pearce to talk, the man would just shut down.

They had been through a lot back in Detroit. Pearce had saved Mark's life, and then Mark had saved Pearce's life, rescuing him from Robert Morgan, the bureau's murderous mole. That was a strong foundation to build a relationship on.

Thoughts of Morgan brought him back to the red Escort, and the knife slipped in Mark's grip, nearly cutting his finger. He put the knife down and closed his eyes for a moment.

"How's that broccoli coming?" Brenda asked.

Mark popped his eyes open and grabbed up the knife once again. Brenda had become increasingly bossy in the past week, never missing a chance to tell him what to do or call him out on a mistake. She had worked for Audra only about two months longer than Mark, but she liked to order Mark around as if she had years more seniority than he did. As a matter of fact, she bossed Darlene around a lot as well, and Darlene had worked for Audra quite a bit longer than the both of them. And Brenda was nosy too. She asked Mark a lot of questions about his living arrangements and background. Sometimes Mark felt as if she was trying to determine his guilt or innocence, though for what crime, he had yet to understand.

"Broccoli's almost done," Mark said.

"Good." Brenda paused across the island from him and frowned down at the stalks of broccoli. "Don't cut the pieces too small, Mark. They're for steaming, not a salad."

Mark nodded once. "Sorry. I got carried away."

Brenda leveled a look at him. "Head in the game, Mark. You heard Audra: this is an important client."

"I know, Brenda. I'm in the game. Don't worry about me."

Brenda watched him a moment before turning back to her own chopping. Mark glared down at the broccoli as if it had betrayed him, then scooped the pieces into a glass storage bowl and turned his thoughts away from Pearce—sexier than anyone had a right to be when he awoke in the mornings—and the mysterious red Escort. He had to focus; he needed this job too much to be so distracted.

124

Click the link to find *Shacked Up* at a number of book retailers: https://books2read.com/shackedup

ABOUT THE AUTHOR

Hank Edwards (he/him) has been writing gay fiction for more than twenty years. He has published over forty novels and novellas and dozens of short stories. His writing crosses many sub-genres, including contemporary romance, rom-com, paranormal, suspense, mystery, wacky comedy, and erotica. He has written a number of series such as the funny and spooky Critter Catchers, Old West historical horror of Venom Valley, suspenseful FBI and civilian Up to Trouble, and the erotic and funny Fluffers, Inc. Under the pen name R. G. Thomas, he has written a young adult urban fantasy gay romance series called The Town of Superstition. He was born and still lives in a northwest suburb of the Motor City, Detroit, Michigan.

For more information:
www.hankedwardsbooks.com
hankedwardsbooks@gmail.com
www.facebook.com/groups/hankshangout

ALSO BY HANK EDWARDS

<u>Critter Catchers Series</u>

Terror by Moonlight

Chasing the Chupacabra

Swamped by Fear

The Devil of Pinesville

Screams of the Season

Horror at Hideaway Cove

Dread of Night

Critter Catchers Box Set 1

Critter Catchers Box Set 2

<u>Critter Catchers Universe Stories</u>

The Mystery of the Morelock Motel

<u>Critter Catchers: Level Up Series</u>

Grave Danger

Wet Screams

<u>Williamsville Inn Gay Romance:</u>

Snowflakes and Song Lyrics

The Cupid Crawl

Fake Date Flip-Flop

Star-Spangled Showdown

<u>**Lacetown Murder Mysteries**</u>

(co-written with Deanna Wadsworth)

Murder Most Lovely

Murder Most Deserving

<u>**Venom Valley Series**</u>

Cowboys & Vampires

Stakes & Spurs

Blood & Stone

<u>**Up to Trouble Series**</u>

Holed Up

Shacked Up

Roughed Up

Choked Up

<u>**Fluffers, Inc. Series**</u>

Fluffers, Inc.

A Carnal Cruise

Vancouver Nights

<u>**Standalone Gay Romance**</u>

Buried Secrets

Destiny's Bastard

Hired Muscle

Plus Ones

Repossession is 9/10ths of the Law

Wicked Reflection

<u>Holiday Gay Romance:</u>

A Gift for Greg (A Story Orgy Single)

Mistletoe at Midnight (A Story Orgy Single)

The Christmas Accomplice

<u>Story Orgy Singles Gay Romance</u>:

A Gift for Greg

By the Book

Cross Country Foreplay

Mistletoe at Midnight

The Cheapskate: Bad Boyfriends

With This Ring

The Story Orgy Singles Boxed Set

<u>The Town of Superstition (YA urban fantasy series)</u>

<u>Published under pen name R. G. Thomas</u>

The Midnight Gardener

The Well of Tears

The Battle of Iron Gulch

A Tangle of Secrets

<u>Gay Erotic Short Story Collections</u>:

A Very Dirty Dozen

Another Very Dirty Dozen

A Third Very Dirty Dozen

A Fourth Very Dirty Dozen

<u>Salacious Singles Gay Erotic Short Stories</u>:

Bear Market

Convoy

Double Down

Exchange Rate

Finding North

Hotel Dick

Kindred Spirits

Sacked

Stroking Midnight

Vanity Loves Company

Wet Lands